# Arizona Heat

## David Huff

Publisher: David Huff
ISBN: 978-0-9988003-0-1
Card Catalogue Number: 2017904541
Arizona Heat/ David Huff
Digital distribution | David Huff, 2017.
Paperback | David Huff | 2017

# DEDICATION

This book is dedicated to my eternal companion and my best friend Linda. She is and always has been the wind beneath my wings. She believed in me even when I didn't believe in myself.

Eternal thought and my guiding star in life:
You and I were never meant to fail.

# CHAPTER I

As Buck stood looking at the brown desert below him that seemed to go on for miles, he was watching for any movement that would give away his quarry. He was searching for anything that would indicate which direction he should go, possibly a dust devil or a whiff of smoke spiraling in the sky that would point him in the right direction to start looking in order to follow the man or maybe men he was after. He wasn't sure at this point of the game; all he knew was that he or they had been involved in a robbery that had gone horribly wrong so wrong that innocent people had been killed, all for being in the wrong place at the wrong time. The robber or robbers had gotten away with the money and stealing a truck nearby to make their escape. Witnesses weren't sure if it had been a one man job or not. Either way, the truck was stolen from the owner as they came out of the bank. Unfortunately, the driver, who put up a fight, wouldn't need it ever again. The old 1999 Ford F-250 Super Duty pickup had room for four or more if they had to ride in the back for a quick getaway. He or they drove to the north end of town missing most of the traffic as they headed out of town following Main Street to the city limits and then cut across the desert to make their getaway. The trail the truck had taken was not much of a trail, more like a bad jeep trail maybe a four-wheeler would use for fun to kill time until something else came along.

The desert was known for hiding all sorts of things, anything from old wagons that didn't or couldn't finish their trek across the godforsaken trails or even the horses or cattle that were used to pull them. Their bones were always not too far from the wagons that didn't finish or live up to their expectations. The whiter the bones the longer they had been in the desert. The rusting junk from old cans and car parts was there as well. All you could see were the barrel cactus and, of course, plenty of prickly pear cactus, which were always around, usually only seen if you walked into a patch of it. Of course, there was life out here; the lizards were always around, and if you looked close enough, you could see their tracks across the dust and sand built up around the sagebrush mounds. Other animals were to be found as well as the occasional road runner and desert fox, along with the jackrabbit, which was always looking for shade.

By the time Buck was put on the case the trail was cold; the wind and sudden downpour the day before covered the tracks that he needed to follow to get the robbers. All he knew for certain was they had started north and were headed across the desert. From there it was anybody's guess. Buck had been one of the original deputies for the Smith County Sheriff's Department. The town of New Rio only required two deputies from Smith County. New Rio was a hole in the wall town and had seen its better days back when the gold rush was hot and going strong. New

Rio was littered by all of the old gold mines below, as well as above. If a person was not careful they could fall into one of the mineshafts by accident, which did happen occasionally.

Now days the only people here were the ones that didn't have enough money to move or they liked being alone out in the middle of nowhere. Buck's family fell into the first group. Buck had gotten the job as a way to stay in the town that he had grown up in. He really didn't care for the town or the people, but it was a job where nothing ever happened until now. Buck considered himself a loner. He liked the desert and when things got bad at home as a kid, usually from the beatings and fights between his parents, Buck would take off into the desert to get away from it. This was his sanctuary from the harsh realities of his life. Only the strong could survive out here. The heat during the summer, which would get up to 120 degrees in the shade, would dry you out so fast that unless you were prepared with plenty of water you could die after only an hour or two of walking around. Without water you would lose your bearings, which would make matters worse. Many had tried, thinking they were prepared to do so. The lucky ones were found wandering without any idea of where they were or where they had been. Others were found later by search parties or by the buzzards flying overhead.

Buck had only one desire and that was to find the man or men responsible for the robbery of the local bank and for the deaths of the truck driver and the teller of the bank. The robbery only netted about fourteen thousand dollars and the truck for what it was worth. Now, as he stood overlooking the valley below him, the wind started blowing across his face. It felt cool, even if it was a hot wind. Being stuck in an oven was something he had gotten used to.

He took his radio and called his position into the sheriff's office to let them know that there was no indication of movement in this area of the desert. Since the holdup the state police had taken over the search.

The state police had their own ways of doing things, as well as their own men. Most of the men from the state police did not want to be out here in the desert. They were not used to the desert heat and wanted their air-conditioned cars and offices. So, of course, when Buck offered to go out into the more remote parts of the desert, they didn't complain at all. They figured that one or two deputies out there were enough to do the job.

The only reason Buck and the other deputy put up with them was for the fact they had the use of a helicopter to cover more ground. But even flying low level you could not see anything of value. There were places to hide such as caves and canyons that would give you shade through the hotter parts of the day. Buck knew of the caves and canyons but with so much desert it was damn near impossible to check every one of them. The chopper was brought in for that. Whether they could see or find anything still remained to be seen.

The dispatcher acknowledged Buck's message and sent him in another direction to check out further west along a ridge of mountains that looked more promising than what he had been looking at. It took about 30 minutes of cross-country driving to get to the base of the ridge. When he finally stopped and started looking around, he headed straight out about a mile from where he parked his truck. The truck was his reference point to the entire desert below the ridge. As long as he kept the truck in sight, he would find his way back.

Two hours later and back at the truck, Buck decided to start climbing up the ridge to get a better view of the area. From a distance the ridge didn't look like it could be climbed. But upon closer scrutiny there were all kinds of places to climb up to the top. You just had to be careful not to lose your footing and fall. The first 500 feet up the ridge, Buck turned to look around and catch his breath. After a moment or two he was able to relax and look more carefully. Out of the corner of his eye he caught the glint of metal shining from the sun. Being part of the old military bombing range, he knew it could be junk left over from that time frame. But he knew it was a possible clue worth checking out.

The binoculars he had with him would show what was what out there. As he raised his glasses to see more clearly, he realized that it was too shiny for anything the military had used. He caught sight of the mirror from a truck. He knew that this could be the vehicle the robbers had taken to get away. The truck looked as if it was a couple miles out from where he stood.

Down below he could see his own truck and from there he could map out a direction to begin making his way to the shiny metal of the truck. He knew the desert could hide gullies and holes that could slow him down, or he might even have to back up and go a different way to get to that same spot he had seen from just below the ridge. He also knew the distance could be greater than he expected it to be; however, that being said, this was the first break the police had had since the robbery. As he carefully drove to where he thought the truck was, he found that the going was pretty good. He was able to catch sight of the truck he had seen and was able to get about one-eighth of a mile away before having to stop and get out to walk the rest of the distance. As Buck got closer to the truck, he realized it was the 1999 Ford Super Duty they had been looking for. He radioed dispatch to let them know he had found the truck. Dispatch said they would pass the message on to the state police and they would be there as soon as possible. At this point all he could do was secure the site and begin looking for anything that would indicate how many were involved and the direction they went.

He looked for all of the telltale signs that would suggest anything out of the ordinary. The bloodstains he saw in the front seat probably belonged to the owner, but the crime-lab persons would be able to confirm this. From what he could tell, the truck had gotten stuck up to its axles in the soft dirt and couldn't go any further. Even the four-wheel-drive option on a vehicle could not have helped in this area of the desert. He could tell there was an oil trail coming out from under the motor of the truck. Buck thought the robbers must have hit a rock or bottomed out and tore a hole in the oil pan in their getaway. As he circled the Ford, he found two sets of tracks leading away from the truck, this time heading east towards the interstate. Buck now realized there were two involved and that they were both on foot.

From the tracks he could tell that one of the men was about six feet and weighed approximately 200 pounds. The second man was shorter and weighed less. Buck wondered how long they could walk in this desert without water or anything else to help them. According to his own calculations, the highway was at least 25 miles from where he found the truck.

The state police helicopter finally showed up about 30 minutes after he radioed in that he had found the truck. Fortunately, the helicopter landed a short distance away from the truck so as not to disturb any tracks on the desert floor that might give them clues or anything else for that matter. Buck thought there may be some hope for these state police actually working with the county to solve this crime.

# Chapter II

Sitting in his chair back in the office, Buck thought they ought to have given the inventor of the air conditioner some kind of award for making life more pleasant. The three hours it took them to get the Ford pickup off the desert and moved to a local garage proved to be a major task. Lucky for them, the cable from the tow truck was long enough to get the stuck vehicle out of the rut it was in. Either way, Buck was appreciative of the coolness of the air-conditioned room.

As he sat at his desk going over the lab reports and crime-scene photos of the robbery, he couldn't help noticing the amount of blood around the body of the teller at the bank. Buck knew the teller just as a friendly face at the bank. Her name was Karen Olds; she had been married for about five years and had one child. Her husband, Jimmy Olds, worked as a traveling salesman gone more often than not. The state police were now trying to track him down to let him know what had happened to his wife. Buck thought to himself, this is one time that he was glad it wasn't him having to break the news of her death to her husband.

The photos showed where Karen's body laid in reference to the spent brass, which was about three feet in front of the body, closer to the door than the victim. The two spent cartridges were from a 9 mil semi-automatic pistol, very effective and accurate at close range for the perpetrator.

The bank in and of itself was considered very small as far as banks go. It had only two teller windows and an office for the manager/loan officer to work from. This bank was attached to another business that sold carpet and linoleum for flooring. There wasn't much room to move around inside the bank, and the basic security was almost nonexistent. Who would have thought that anybody in the town of New Rio would rob the bank?

As Buck continued reading the crime reports, something did not add up and left him more perplexed than ever. There had been no need to kill the teller. According to the witnesses at the scene, it seemed as if the teller had been shot as an afterthought. Evidently, the money had already been handed out and the robbers were on their way out the door when the teller was shot. Buck thought to himself, why kill someone when you didn't need to, especially when it now became armed robbery/murder with a guaranteed 20 years to life imprisonment versus five to ten years for robbery without a gun.

Buck decided to look into the background of the Olds family. Jim and Karen Olds were born in Phoenix and went to high school in South Glendale. Jim was the class jock who had lettered in football and basketball and had received a scholarship to play football at Arizona State University. Karen was on the cheerleading squad and was by all accounts to be Jim's sweetheart.

They went to Arizona State University where Jim majored in business and marketing while he played football. Karen took classes in managerial accounting and administration. They married in their second year of college; it seemed the ideal situation for both of them. Jim's scholarship went away after he blew out his knee his third year from a bad tackle, which forced him to land on his knee the wrong way. Jim was forced to find a job while going to school to pay for their new baby who was on its way. Karen left school after their son was born to stay home and take care of the new baby.

By all accounts Jim and Karen were happy in spite of the long hours Jim had to spend working to support himself and his family. Finishing college Jim landed a job working as a road warrior for Ace Electronics Corporation selling secure radio communications systems and the hardware that went with it. This paid very well for about a year and a half until the bottom fell out of the industry. Jim was forced to find any kind of job just to make ends meet. This had included working at a local grocery store as an assistant manager and as a car salesman. These jobs paid very little when compared to what he had been making with Ace Electronics Corp. Through it all they ended up in New Rio and had been there for the last two years. Jim found a job where he was once more a district manager for a company based in Phoenix similar to Ace Electronics. Karen found a job at the bank as a part-time teller, where she could be at home enough to raise their son. She had been working at the bank for at least a year.

The driver of the pickup, Curt Simms, who had been shot, was a longtime resident who owned a small cattle ranch, which had never taken off. Yet it was enough for the old man to pay his bills and live comfortably for the last 50 years or so. He had no children, leastwise none that Buck could remember; they had either moved away or were never there. The old man was a loner of sorts, stayed to himself, only coming into town as needed for supplies. Neither Karen nor Curt had anything in common, except being at the wrong place at the wrong time. Buck was trying to figure out the whys and wherefores for the bank robbery and any connection to the victims, questioning himself as to whether they were random or premeditated acts.

The bank in and of itself was not known for having large amounts of money on hand at any time, with no real business industry in the area which would require large sums of money just to cash the employees' checks. It was more like a mom and pop store that catered to the small businesses that barely existed to support the townsfolk.

By now the state police had finished their forensics inspection of the pickup truck left by the robbers. All they could ascertain was the blood in the truck matched the owner, Curt Sims, and the few fingerprints found were hard to read as to be of any use. With no one there to claim the pickup, it would be sold for parts and whatever they could get out of it to pay the towing bill. With the exception of the two sets of tracks heading east to the highway, they had no leads to follow. The state police followed the tracks which they assumed went in the direction of the interstate, and realized that the tracks disappeared before getting there.

Buck thought to himself that he needed to go back into the desert and follow the tracks himself. Maybe, just maybe, he might find something that the state police missed in their search. He would go early the next morning and take a look for himself.

After talking to the state police superintendent, Dan Foster, he let him know that he was going back out into the desert to do his own search of the area. Dan looked at him for a second and not wanting to spend any more time or man hours, which equated to money, said, "Good luck and good hunting."

# Chapter III

At 5:00 am the next morning Buck was at the location where they had found the Ford pickup. In the early morning light he was able to find the two sets of footprints that led away from the pickup. For the first part of the search they were easy to follow, heading east towards the highway as he thought they would be doing. Towards noon the tracks headed into a rocky area, where the robbers could hide their tracks and still move without being followed by stepping on the rocks and going in any direction they chose.

It took another hour to pick up the tracks again. Buck had walked a large circle around the last set of good prints to find where they picked up again. By doing so he found only one set of tracks, not the two as before. This meant one of the men involved was still out here somewhere in the rocky area.

To Buck, this was getting more interesting all the time. Where had the second person gone? Was he dead or did he get his cut of the money and take off on his own, maybe back into New Rio? Not knowing for sure, Buck knew he would be out all night and part of tomorrow trying to figure it out. Buck decided to take a closer look at the rocky area, hoping he would find the second set of tracks.

Going back and forth in a straight line from one end to the other, halfway across the rocky area he found what he was looking for: a crevasse big enough to hide in and deep enough to be not seen from above. This would have provided shelter and shade for whoever needed it without being found. From all appearances it looked like a shadow on the rocky outcropping. Buck shined his flashlight into the crevasse as he scanned the area from above. At first he didn't see anything, but the second scan caught the reflection of something that was manmade. Not knowing what it was, he decided he would have to go down into the crevasse. Climbing down through the opening into the darkness was a little unnerving.

Peering down into the darkness, Buck's eyes acclimated to the bottom of the crevasse. The handholds and footholds made it easy to get through the opening. When he touched the ground again, he used his flashlight to get an idea of the size of the opening. As he peered into the darkness, the crevasse was about the size of a small cave, about 6 x 8 feet, and he was able to stand without having to bend over to move around.

Something had been down in here, who or what it was Buck wasn't sure. Following his light across the floor, he found what he had seen above. It was a belt buckle still attached to pants. A man's body was lying out as if resting for a moment, as if he were catching his breath. Upon a closer look, he could tell the man was dead; the bullet hole in the front of his head was quick to see. The look on the man's face was a surprised look, as if he wasn't expecting it. Buck did not recognize him as a local and started searching his body for any identification as to who he was. He found his wallet but any identification was gone; even his credit cards were missing. Fingerprints would tell who he was. Buck realized he needed to get the body back to the station to do this.

Around the body were some dollar bills. Buck thought it was probably some money from the bank. The serial numbers on the bills would prove or disprove this. He gathered the money together and stuffed it into his shirt pocket. Now, how to get this guy out of this hole and through the crevasse. Buck wished he had a rope, which would have made it a lot easier. The rope, of course, was back in the truck box in the bed of the truck. He thought to himself, a nice place to have it when you need it. Buck looked around the cave and didn't see anything that would or could help him in his predicament. He thought he would have to leave the body and go get the rope. It wasn't like the body was going anywhere; it had already been there two days. Daylight was fading fast into the west when he got out of the crevasse. He headed towards his truck to get the rope to pull out the body. Buck knew it would be tough going in the dark to try and find the crevasse again, so he decided to wait for the morning light to find the crevasse. Buck pulled out his blanket and curled up into the cab of his truck and tried to sleep.

# CHAPTER IV

After getting the body back to the medical examiner's office for an autopsy and turning in the money he found next to the body, Buck was able to go home and clean up. After shaving and taking a shower, not only did he smell better but he felt better. While there he checked his phone for any messages; there were none that couldn't wait until he headed back into the sheriff's office.

Dan Foster was waiting for him when he arrived. "Where did you find him?"

Buck told him about the crevasse and how he had to go down into it to find the body and then drag him out the next morning. Dan was amazed that he found anything out there. Foster let Buck know that they were running his fingerprints through the FBI database to figure out who this guy was.

No one recognized the body, in spite of the decomposition. Buck did not recognize him as a local or, for that matter, a transient. This really caused some concern to both Foster and Buck. Just who was this guy, where did he come from, and, most of all, who was his partner and why did they rob this bank? This had Buck wondering if there were some shenanigans going on at the bank. After talking to Foster about his concerns, Foster agreed to look into the bank for any irregularities regarding how much money the bank actually handles on a regular basis. Buck figured that the state police superintendent had enough clout to go ahead and get permission for an audit. At this point Buck was waiting for the answers, and he knew it would take some time to get them.

"I'm going home to get some sleep in a real bed instead of the cab of my truck," Buck told Foster.

"If anything comes up I'll call you and let you know," Foster assured Buck.

With that Buck went home.

The phone rang the next morning about 8:00, Buck answered it as he lay in bed; it was Foster. After the good morning chit chat, Foster let him know they got information from the FBI about the fingerprints. Foster asked Buck to get with him when he came in. Buck showed up about 9:00 and, with a cup of coffee in his hand, went to see Foster.

Foster was sitting at one of the makeshift desks in the room they had been using as a command center. When Buck walked in, Foster met him halfway with the report from the FBI in his hand. "Take a look at this report."

Buck looked over the report and was still not sure what to make of it. The fingerprints identified the man out of Chicago as George Whitey, a low-level thug with ties to the Midwest Syndicate. The money that Buck turned in with the body also came back with the serial numbers matching another robbery in Denver six months earlier.

"What do you think?" Foster asked Buck.

Buck looked at him with a puzzled look. "I don't know what to make of this. This doesn't make any sense at all. Why would a thug working for a crime organization in Chicago be in New Rio to rob a bank for fourteen thousand dollars? Where is the connection and who is the other accomplice to the robbery?"

Foster and Buck were standing there when the medical examiner showed up.

"The gunshot is obviously what killed the guy. But the other information gleaned from the exam showed that George was in the final stages of liver cancer," Dr. Davis told them.

Foster thought that maybe George Whitey must have had a death wish before dying to be rich and to live out his final days in luxury.

"Maybe we can track down and locate the doctor from his old stomping grounds in Chicago who diagnosed him with the cancer," Buck said.

"I'll check into that angle and see what I can find," Foster said.

"And I'll head back to the bank and check with the auditors to see if anything new turned up from the records check," Buck said.

Buck crossed the street. It was already noon and it was hot and dry; it was going to be another hot scorcher in New Rio, Arizona. He made his way to the bank, thinking to himself about the new-found evidence and trying to make sense of it all. Something, of course, didn't fit; but what was the key to it all? Buck reached the bank and opened the door to walk in. The coolness of the AC felt good to him. He made his way back to the bank manager's office. When he got there, the manager wasn't there. The bank manager had showed up earlier the day before after hearing about the bank being robbed. Buck looked for the auditor and finally found him inside the bank teller's area. The auditor was quietly working on his notes and records in front of him and did not notice Buck standing there. He worked for another five minutes before he looked up and realized Buck had been standing there watching him work. The auditor came from behind the teller's cage and motioned Buck into the bank manager's office. The auditor made himself at home in the chair behind the desk and proceeded to unload all of his notes to give Buck a review of what he had found. Buck pulled up a chair opposite the auditor and waited for him to start.

The auditor started slow, pausing to take a breath before getting into the meat and potatoes of his notes. "The bank records checked out okay at first glance; however, the amount of money going through the bank doesn't match the amount coming in. It was impossible to tell at first, but small amounts were being added as deposits from outside the valley, not significant amounts but constant enough to have a pattern. First it was 500 dollars once a month to as much as ten thousand dollars twice a month. This has been going on for about three years."

"Who's making the deposits?" Buck asked.

"The money is coming from the Smith-field Construction Company," the auditor answered.

Buck thought for a moment about the construction company. He remembered working there as a kid part time in high school and selling the materials to build homes and commercial buildings. He also knew the owners on a first-name basis and went to school with one of the owners' kids. However, the Smithfield Construction Company went out of business a couple years ago due to hiring illegals and getting caught by Department of Homeland Security (DHS).

Buck thought it strange that a defunct company was still making money and depositing it into the bank.

"I need you to go back into the records and find or locate any other large deposits made for the last ten years, and create a list of companies for me to check into," Buck said.

"It will take some time but I can do it," said the auditor.

With this new information Buck walked back to the sheriff's office. He gave the new information the auditor had given him to Foster, who looked at him in surprise.

After shaking his head, he looked at Buck. "The fun just keeps coming our way."

Buck just shook his head in agreement.

"Maybe we could have the FBI come in to help with the investigation, might be a good thing," Foster said.

"I concur."

Foster contacted the Phoenix Office of the FBI and basically told them what was going on with the robbery in New Rio and how they had found money matching a robbery that occurred in Denver, and also how they had found a trail of money going into the bank which couldn't be accounted for.

The FBI agent in charge, Silas Brown, said, "I'll be sending out someone in the next day or two after closing up a few matters we have been working on in the Phoenix area. Do you have any information on which drug cartel is involved in the robbery?"

"I have no idea at this point and I was hoping that The FBI could shed some light on this for me."

"I will bring any information we have with me."

All Buck and Foster could do at this time was wait and see what else the auditor came up with, hoping it would lead to other people that might know more and give more information to solve this case.

Buck decided to head back out into the desert to see if he could find any other information or clue that would help. He asked Foster to see if he was interested in going out with him. Foster looked at him and thought to himself what else could they do except wait here and do nothing.

"Yeah, let's go," Foster said.

Once back in the desert, Buck showed Foster where the crevasse was and where he found the body. Foster looked down inside the cave from above and started going down inside the opening. Once Buck was inside the cave as well, they started looking around. They weren't sure what they were looking for, but as the saying goes, they would know it once they saw it. After searching around for about 30 minutes they found nothing except where the body had been laying.

When they were topside again, they continued to look around the opening of the crevasse. They found a set of footprints leading away from the rocky area, headed in the direction of the interstate. After following the tracks for about a mile, they stopped. At this point a new set of tire tracks appeared, which headed south back into the desert.

"The border to Mexico is only an hour away in that direction by vehicle. There may have been a third person involved, or maybe the vehicle was parked there so the robber could make his way across the desert to get to Mexico," Buck told Foster.

As usual, this brought more questions than answers.

They made their way back to their own truck and talking amongst themselves they decided to follow the tracks they had found in order to see where they led. After following the tracks for some three miles, they found a dirt trail that turned into a road. No doubt Buck and Foster had found an unknown entrance way for the drug mules and illegals to get into the U.S. without being caught. Buck thought to himself that he needed to annotate the map on the wall in the office about this new trail. There were plenty of empty water jugs and clothes and other paraphernalia lying about indicating activity around the trail. The robber must have known this and had used this same route to get across the border undetected. DHS would have to be contacted and made aware of the new trail once they got back to New Rio.

Once they got to the Mexican border, they found a small, sparsely populated village. The village looked more like a watering hole for the local farmers than a thoroughfare headed to all of old Mexico. The tracks they had followed were lost amongst the other vehicle tracks on the main road, as it was; it looked like another dead end. The only thing they knew for sure was the robber got away with murder and money and that it was a lot of work to go through for fourteen thousand dollars.

There had to have been more going on but what it was, they could only guess. They made their way back across the border to the American side and followed their own trail back to where they had started. Once there Buck and Foster drove back to New Rio, all in all about eight hours in the desert for nothing.

Foster started talking first when they reached the office, more thinking out loud than anything else; "There had to have been more money involved in the robbery than what was officially stated. Now the question is, how much and from whom?"

"Which only the auditor can answer," said Buck.

# CHAPTER V

The following day the FBI showed up about 10:00 am. Upon their arrival Foster and Buck were eager to learn what and if the FBI had any information that was pertinent to their case. The first Special Agent, Rachael Adams, was an attractive brunette, about 5′ 9″, she had piercing blue eyes and a no nonsense air about her. You could tell Special Agent Rachael Adams was all business. Her partner, Jim Evans, was a little less business like but still intimidating with his black suit and sunglasses. He stood 6′ 3″ and weighed about 220 pounds; he wore glasses and his hair was completely white. Looking at the two of them, Buck thought to himself, "You would think that they were working for a major crime family themselves." Once the pleasantries were done, they all went into an adjoining room to discuss what they had learned about the case.

It was Special Agent Evans who spoke first. He explained that they had been tracking George Whitey all the way from Chicago. He was wanted or suspected for racketeering and murder for hire and the organization who hired him had promoted George Whitey to outfit street boss a couple years back. The problem was that Whitey had gotten greedy with his boss's money and Whitey had taken off with two hundred grand and was on the run. He had robbed the bank in Denver for some chump change to see himself off to Mexico. Sammy the Freak, the Chicago boss, had put out a quarter million dollar contract out on him.

Evidently, Whitey had wanted to turn himself in to the FBI and work as an informant and key witness against the crime family.

"We were in the process of picking him up when Whitey found out he had cancer and disappeared on us. His partner, Ken Ritchins, was a kid he had picked up for the Denver robbery and had decided to tag along with him," Special Agent Evans stated.

"How did you find George Whitey?" Special Agent Rachael Adams asked.

"He had been involved in the bank robbery here in New Rio and had been found shot to death in the desert afterwards," Foster said.

The two FBI agents looked at each other and, after looking at the photos that the medical examiner had given to Foster, confirmed it was Whitey.

"How much money was taken in the New Rio robbery?" Evans asked.

"14 K," Buck replied.

"Why would Whitey need to rob the bank in Denver and New Rio if he was carrying close to a quarter million dollars with him?" Rachael asked.

"Maybe he wanted to be caught with the money," Foster answered.

They all agreed that they needed to find Ritchins, his partner, to answer that question. Agent Evans called his office and put out a BOLO (Be On the Look Out) for Ritchins in old Mexico and the surrounding areas. Evans thought it was a long shot but under these circumstances it was a start, besides what else could they do? Afterwards Buck took the agents back out into the desert to show them where the truck had been found and where he had found Whitey's body. Foster didn't go with them due to other issues that had come up. Besides, he had seen the place earlier and another trek into the desert was not what he had in mind for fun.

By the time Buck and the agents returned it was late in the afternoon. He dropped the agents off where their car was parked and headed home. Sitting in front of the air conditioner, trying to cool down with a cold drink in his hand, Buck heard a knock on the door. He opened the door and there stood agent Adams. Buck was surprised to see her standing at the door; it took a minute to realize who she was. She had changed her clothes and her hair was not tied up in a bun.

Buck wondered what she was doing there and asked, "Can I help you with anything?"

At first she studied him and then asked, "Is this a bad time?"

"No, I'm just surprised to see you here."

"I was hungry and wanted to know where there was a good place to eat dinner."

Buck thought for a moment and said, "The café on Main Street serves a mean hamburger with fries that are the talk of the town." He hadn't eaten yet so they both went to dinner.

While eating Rachael Adams asked him how long he had been a deputy and if he liked the job. Buck told her that he had graduated from high school and had gone to ASU in Phoenix for a couple of years on a scholarship to play football. He had been hit hard in the knees in one of the games and lost his scholarship due to a knee surgery that had sidelined him for football. With no money for school he had come home back to New Rio looking for work and ended up getting a job as a deputy for the county.

Rachael said she had started out wanting to be an attorney at first but liked the idea of being an agent and catching bad guys for the FBI. She had applied while in her senior year at college and had been accepted. She went to the FBI Academy and was made an agent four years ago. This was her first assignment working out of the office in Phoenix in the white collar crime division. Watching the actions of Mafia hit men and dons who had retired to live out their days in Phoenix hadn't been all that exciting, so when this came open she had volunteered to go with Agent Evans.

After dinner they headed back to his place and sat and talked a little more. Rachael reached out and took his hand and thanked him for his company at dinner; she then said good night as he walked her to her car. He walked back to his place, sat down and thought how nice it was to go on a date once again. As he thought about Rachael, he smiled to himself and sat down in front of the air conditioner and turned on the television.

The next morning Buck arrived at the office as usual and looked over the reports to see if anything had happened while he was off duty. There had been some vandalism to one of the local shops. Some kids had sprayed graffiti on the doors of the local drug store near the high school, more of a nuisance than a crime but nowadays still had to be reported. Buck got hold of Foster to see if anything new had been reported about the robbery/murders and if any information about Ritchins had surfaced. Foster replied that nothing had turned up and that Ritchins could be in China by now. The FBI agents were hunting for Ritchins as well, but Buck wondered how long they would be in New Rio before heading back to Phoenix.

Agents Evans and Adams came in carrying their own cups of coffee and looking all the part of being FBI agents dressed in the suits and sunglasses. Buck was surprised to see the transformation of agent Adams from last night to now. He would have never guessed that she was an agent from what she had worn the night before. Agent Evans was the first to speak about Ritchins being seen in the border town of Nogales, Mexico. The Mexican police had reported him to their own FBI counter-parts and that they had picked him up and had him incarcerated in one of their jail cells as a goodwill gesture towards the American FBI.

Agents Evans and Adams left later that afternoon to bring Ritchins back to New Rio for more questioning and to charge him for the robbery of the bank and the murders of Karen Olds and Curt Sims.

Buck was thinking as he looked at Foster, who was thinking the same thing, finally a break in the case. Something tangible they could pursue and hopefully get some answers to help solving this case.

Later that afternoon Jim Olds, Karen's husband, had come in to find out what had happened to his wife. You could tell it had been rough on him. He had just come from the medical examiner's office to identify the body. Foster saw him first and motioned him into one of the interrogation rooms; Buck followed them into the room as well. Buck looked at Jim and could tell it had been hard on him to find out that his wife was gone and that he was now all alone to raise their son. The boy had been taken care of by some neighbors until Jim could be home. Buck thought for a moment, what would Jim do? Would he leave New Rio or pick up the pieces and stay here? Anybody's guess, but one Buck hoped he would never have to make for himself.

Looking at Jim he could tell he hadn't slept in a while and that he was still in a state of shock about his wife's death. Jim was trying to hold it together for his son's sake. Just how long that would be was anybody's guess. By this time Buck thought to himself that he was glad he wasn't married yet. Watching Jim, all he saw was a broken man who had his world turned upside down and inside out. After viewing the body and signing some paperwork to release the body, Foster escorted Jim to the front door and shared his condolences once more and left him.

Foster asked Buck about the auditor he had talked with earlier in the week and thought it might be a good idea to get back with him. Buck had almost forgotten about the audit that was going on in the bank and agreed to go check it out. Upon reaching the bank he could not find the auditor inside. After asking one of the other tellers, Buck found him in the vault looking around inside with a perplexed look on his face.

"Hello and why such a look of concern on your face?" Buck said.

"I'm looking for a safety deposit box that is supposed to have a lot of money inside it. The safety deposit box is numbered 1001, yet there are only 100 safety deposit boxes inside the vault. According to the bank records there has been approximately 250,000 dollars deposited into this box," the auditor explained.

Buck called Foster about the auditor's concerns and shortly Foster was there looking over the shoulder of the auditor and looking at the bank records himself. Both of them realized something was wrong and that they would need a warrant to proceed any further. Buck asked the auditor to double-check his work and send him a report showing what he had found in the bank's records, especially the missing safety deposit box, the money supposed to be in the box, and a list of all the names of the safety deposit box holders. The auditor said he should be able to complete it in a couple of hours and the report would be sent to him later that day.

Foster and Buck walked and talked all the way back to their office about the missing money and safety-deposit box. They both thought maybe this bank was being used to launder money from the drug cartels. But without some kind of proof, all they could do was speculate. Foster said he would get in touch with FBI agents Evans and Adams and that he would request a warrant with the district attorney to start looking a little closer into the bank records. All of this would take some time but, as it was, it was the only thing they had to go on.

The FBI agents showed up two days later with Ritchins in tow. Ritchins looked as if he'd been out all night partying and barely gotten home to sleep. You could tell

Evans and Rachael were both tired themselves but you couldn't really tell that until they took their aviator sunglasses off. Evans was happy they had Ritchins and escorted him to a holding cell and locked him in. Evans asked who wanted to watch the interrogation up close and personal as he had planned on asking Ritchins himself first about the robbery and then the murders. Rachael and Evans fixed themselves some more coffee, this time no cream or sugar, just straight, so that they would be awake for the answers they were hoping to get from Ritchins on his part in the robbery and murders.

When being questioned by the FBI agents while in Mexico, Ritchins refused to confirm he was one of the robbers, let alone one of the murderers. He hadn't even talked while being transferred back to New Rio. The FBI office in Denver had a file on Ritchins and sent it to Evans for a review. No telling what they would find in it. Rachael was the profiler of the two agents. Hopefully she would be able to put something together that would get

Ritchins to crack, telling them what had happened. Hopefully, the first crack would be when the other bank employees could identify him as one of the robbers.

Once Rachael and Evans were brought up to speed about the money in the safety-deposit box and how much money was unaccounted for, they agreed the bank needed a closer look. Buck apprised them of the warrant and what he had already started with the auditor.

Rachael exclaimed joking, "You didn't need us to hold your hand for this?"

Buck rolled his eyes and laughed. "I thought about calling you FBI guys because without adult supervision we were scared to act on our own."

Both agents and Foster laughed, thinking one point for their team. Evans feigned hurt feelings and Rachael couldn't help but smile.

The auditor showed up with his findings about the money and the list of names that had safety-deposit boxes inside the bank. The report confirmed what the auditor had said earlier; a quarter of a million dollars was missing and the safety-deposit box was nowhere to be found. The list of names with safety-deposit boxes had to have background checks done to verify their innocence. This would take some time to confirm. Fortunately, computers would save a lot of time and effort in running background checks on the individuals with boxes.

By this time everybody was anxious to interrogate Ritchins about his part in the robbery and subsequent murders. The FBI would take the lead in part of the investigation and the others would watch from behind the two-way mirror. In the meantime the bank personnel were being brought to the station hopefully to identify the bank robber. The bank employees were brought in one at a time and would watch from behind the two-way mirror to see if they could identify Ritchins as one of the robbers. Buck was hoping that one of the employees would be able to identify Ritchins as one of the robbers.

While Ritchins waited for the interrogation to begin, each one of the bank personnel got to get a good look at him. They all agreed that Ritchins was one of the robbers from the holdup. One down, two to go, to seal Ritchins fate.

Once the FBI had confirmation on Ritchins as one of the bank robbers, they went to work interrogating him. They were hoping that he was just as tired as the interrogators were and that would be an advantage for them and that he would break down easier. With Buck and Foster watching from behind the two-way mirror the agents walked into the room where Ritchins was sitting.

# CHAPTER VI

Ritchins had been sitting for about an hour inside the interrogation room waiting for the FBI to show up. Having fallen asleep while waiting for them, he was startled awake when they came in. Rachael asked Ritchins if they bothered him by interrupting his nap time. Ritchins looked at her and laughed. The interrogation questions started coming hard and fast; Rachael went first, then Evans asking the same questions: What went wrong with him killing his partner, Whitey? How much money did you guys really get? What were you planning on doing in Mexico? Where were you headed after Mexico? Where is the money you guys had stolen? Both Evans and Rachael were asking faster than Ritchins could answer. After about approximately three hours of double teaming him, Ritchins started sweating. Rachael and Evans had Ritchins where they wanted him, the good cop bad cop routine then started.

Rachael was the good cop trying to soothe Ritchins by offering him water and a sandwich, while Evans was pounding his fist on the table in the room, threatening him with the needle and at least life with no parole in the maximum-security prison, unless he told them what he wanted to know. First, Evans would be kicked out of the interrogation room by Rachael for almost losing it, while Rachael would try to calm Ritchins down by not allowing Evans to come back into the interrogation room. Evans would wait five minutes and come back in and say that whatever Rachael was promising couldn't be done, especially for him. Always looking into the folder, they had on Ritchins, the pictures from the crime scene were laid out. The lifeless bodies of the teller and the truck driver were lying on the table. Evans would force Ritchins to look at the photos and threaten him with the needle.

Ritchins kept saying that he didn't kill either the girl at the bank or the old man with the truck. Evans said it didn't matter, he was still going down for the murders anyway, armed robbery carried a minimum of 20 years in prison, no matter what. Ritchins stated how he was surprised by the way Whitey was acting; it was as though he was crazy and nothing could stop him. Ritchins kept saying that Whitey was always taking some kind of pills to keep him going, and that he tried to stop Whitey from shooting the teller. It was as if the female teller knew who Whitey was. Whitey shoved Ritchins away and almost shot him for getting in his way. It was if he was on auto-pilot and that nothing could stop him. The old man was at the wrong place at the wrong time and started to fight with Whitey about him taking his truck; consequently, he was shot for his truck in order that they could make the getaway. The truck was closer than their car when they came out of the bank.

By now both Evans and Rachael were seated at the opposite side of the table listening to what Ritchins was saying. Evans asked why he had shot Whitey in the cave.

Ritchins claimed it was in self-defense; Whitey tried to shoot him while they were in the cave. Ritchins took the money and got out of the cave. The plan had included an ATV waiting for them that would take them across the desert to the town just the other side of the border. The truck broke down before they could get to the ATV and they had to hole up somewhere away from the truck and from there make their way to the ATV. Rachael asked him once again how much money they had taken from the holdup. Ritchins replied 200 K was their haul. Both Rachael and Evans looked at each other trying to figure out why so much, when the bank reported only 14, 000 dollars was missing. Now again, there were more questions than answers. At this time there was a knock at the door to the interrogation room.

Rachael opened the door and stepped out.

"Don't leave me here alone with Evans," Ritchins cried.

Rachael laughed inside, knowing Ritchins was truly afraid of Evans. It was

Buck who had just reviewed the information from the auditor at the bank. By this time Evans came out of the room and was standing there waiting to hear what Buck had found out. Buck explained that from the looks of it the bank was laundering money for one of the Mexican drug cartels and that Whitey knew this and had waited for the right time to rob the bank to get the laundered money. It was supposed to be the last big score for Whitey before he died from the cancer.

Evans and Rachael went back into the interrogation room and asked Ritchins how Whitey knew about the laundered money being in the bank. Ritchins explained that Whitey's job was to make sure the money that needed to be laundered was sent there. Evidently, Whitey's job for the crime family was as a courier for the money to the bank. The teller, Karen Olds, was the point of contact for the drop-off. She was to take the money as a deposit from Whitey and put it into a special account set up just for the dirty money. She then would slowly put the money back into circulation with the evening deposits from the Smithfield Construction Company. With this new information Rachael came out of the room and asked for Buck and Foster to run a thorough background check on the finances of Jim and Karen Olds, the Smith Construction Company and anybody else they could think of. Foster got right on it and Buck went back to the bank to talk to the people who worked at the bank who knew Karen Olds. The loan officer, Mary Donaldson, was the first person that Buck talked to about Karen. Mary really knew very little about Karen, other than they went to lunch together once a week. When asked about her personal life Mary said that Karen was always complaining about being bored in a small town with nothing to do. She had missed the night life of Phoenix and wished she could go back to it. Mary was surprised to hear about the money laundering part that Karen had done. However, that being said, Mary also thought it was customary for Karen to do the final tally for the bank deposits at night. Karen had been offered other positions at the other branches where the banks were located, but she had always turned them down. Mary thought it odd that Karen missed the night life in the big city, yet when offered a chance to go there she always turned it down. She would always say it was Jim, her husband, who would say no about these new opportunities.

After Buck finished his talk with Mary, he then talked to the auditor about this new information and asked him to look into the bank accounts of Jim and Karen Olds. Buck's next stop was to visit with Jim Olds. Jim was easy to follow up on as he had to prepare for the funeral for his wife and also having to be there for their son. He found Jim talking to the mortician about a casket for Karen and a plot for her to be buried in. The boy was being entertained by the mortician's secretary. Buck sat back and watched Jim with a renewed interest to see if there were any telltale signs of Jim's involvement with the bank robbery and murder of his wife. Jim looked as if he was having a hard time with all of this.

Buck kind of felt sorry for him having to go through all of this for someone he had cared about. Buck wasn't sure he could have done better. After about 15 minutes of watching Jim signing the paperwork, he had arranged everything needed to bury his wife. With that being done Buck walked up to him and offered his condolences and asked how he was doing. Jim was surprised to see Buck there and was not sure what to make of it. Buck said he had some questions for Jim to answer and wondered if this was a good time to do so. Jim watched his son with the secretary playing and laughing; the boy had not understood about his mother not coming back. The boy knew that his mother had gone far away and didn't know when she would return.

Jim sat back in the mortician's office with Buck asking the questions. At first Jim answered quickly, but when asked about Karen's bank job, Jim stopped and looked at Buck for a minute. He started realizing this wasn't just a friendly visit but an interrogation into Karen's work habits. Jim asked Buck why he was asking all of the questions about Karen's bank Job. Buck stated it was just a matter of routine questions and that he was following up to clarify a few key points that had come up in their investigation of the bank robbery. Jim knew this wasn't the truth, but what was he to do? At this point Jim asked Buck if he was a suspect in the bank robbery and should he get a lawyer. Buck replied no to the questions, stating that Jim had been out of the area when the robbery and murders occurred. Buck reassured Jim once more that the questions were routine. He asked Jim how things were between him and Karen.

Buck continued with the basic questions of issues dealing with money or their marriage that would indicate problems inside or outside the normal realm. Jim replied that, at first, when they moved here money was always short and the times were hard until Karen was able to get hired at the bank in New Rio. The stress of not enough money seemed to have a snowball effect into every aspect of their lives. With the new job the stress seemed to be gone. At this juncture Buck's cell phone rang; he politely excused himself to take the call. Buck went into the adjacent room to have some privacy. It was Foster who was calling. Foster told him that the auditor found a discrepancy in Jim and Karen's bank account. They had approximately 40 thousand dollars in their savings account and 10 thousand dollars in their checking account. Foster was surprised at the amount in the accounts simply because it showed the money had been deposited in the last 10 months. Buck thought to himself, that's a hell of a pay raise for working at a bank that barely pays above minimum wage. Buck asked where the money was deposited from. Foster said he didn't know but they were cash deposits in increments of two to three thousand dollars each month.

With this new information about the money in the bank, Jim became a possible suspect in Karen's murder. Buck asked

Foster to go back and look into Jim's records and keep digging.

"Way ahead of you, will let you know what I find," Foster replied.

When Buck returned, Jim was still there. Buck apologized about the interruption and sat down. He started asking Jim about unusual behavior that he might have seen from Karen. Jim stated that with him being a road warrior and being gone most of the time, he couldn't tell him anything definite. Jim did say that every once in a while new things would appear like new furniture and clothes for her. Karen would always say it was a bonus from work. Not thinking anymore about, it he accepted it as truth. Buck thought to himself about all of this as being a coincidence, or maybe he was into it as well. Buck made a mental note to tell Foster to look into the route that Jim took for his job.

Buck asked what kind of salesman he was and what he sold. Jim told Buck that he was a district manager for an electronics company based in Phoenix. He covered the southern part of Arizona handling distribution and sales in that area. Jim told him he sold radios for business vehicles and for personal use as well. The job wasn't as good as his first job, but it paid the bills. For Jim it was a comfortable living, especially for living in New Rio. The cost of living in Phoenix had not gotten to New Rio yet. Buck asked if they provided a car for him to travel while working. He replied yes and that it wasn't much for all the travelling he was doing. Buck thought that there wasn't anything out of place about Jim or his job. So with that, he got up and thanked him for his time and then headed back to the office.

Buck headed back to the sheriff's office wondering about Jim's involvement in his wife's death. Was there a connection? Was he part of the plan of drug smuggling or money laundering, or was he innocent? With all of these questions rolling around in his head, Buck went to look for Foster.

Buck caught up with Foster as soon as he got to his office. Foster was looking at some paperwork when Buck walked over to him.

"Is there anything new to report?" Buck asked.

"The records I found on Jim and Karen Olds were how you would say interesting, to say the least. Jim would always take his road trips the day after the money was deposited from the Smith Construction Company. He would be gone on these trips about a week at a time," Foster replied.

"Were you able to determine if the trips would always go to the same places?"

Foster was looking at Jim's travel records, "It looks that way. His travels always started in Phoenix via Nogales, Tucson, Yuma, and then back to Phoenix, and from Phoenix he would head back to New Rio."

"We better let Rachael and Evans in on what we found out."

Rachael was the first to respond when Buck and Foster told them about Jim's travels.

"We need to get ahold of the company that Jim works for to verify not only what Jim does for them but also where he does it for them," Rachael said.

"Simple enough to check out with a phone call to the company," Evans said. With that, he and Rachael headed out the door.

By now it had been a week and still nothing per se to connect the pieces together for the robbery and murders to anyone. They had Ritchins for both the robbery and the murders but with no real solid evidence to hold Ritchins. All they could charge him with would be armed robbery.

Buck thought that something was missing in this case. Nobody was supposed to get killed in the robbery, yet this is exactly what happened. The last thing the bad guys wanted in this situation was to have its cover blown. Buck wondered how long the money laundering had really been going on. If it was a money-laundering operation for the syndicate they wouldn't want it known. How did Jim and Karen fit in? Was it just the money or were there drugs involved as well. More questions than answers; hopefully, Rachael and Evans would turn something up. From the outset this situation was unusual, to say the least. All major law enforcement agencies were involved in trying to put the pieces together. Buck kept thinking that there was more behind all of this. Just what it was he wasn't sure. He chuckled as he was halfway expecting that the CIA and any of the other alphabets would be the next player coming in to introduce themselves.

# CHAPTER VII

The next day Buck went back to the bank and started talking to the employees that were there during the robbery. He had already interviewed Mary, the loan officer. Who else would have been there at the time of the robbery? He looked for Mary to see if she knew the answer to this. Buck found Mary as she was talking to one of their bank customers. He waited patiently till the customer left.

Upon leaving Mary asked, "How may I help you?"

"Can you remember who was working the day the robbery occurred?" Buck asked.

Mary thought for a moment. "There was one other person there at the time of the robbery, Bill or rather William Garner. He left earlier that same day to run some personal errands at lunchtime just before the robbery took place."

"Is Bill anywhere around?"

"No, he went to an appointment this morning before coming in to work. Because of the robbery Bill has started seeing a counselor to help him deal with what happened at the bank that day."

Mary claimed that Bill had been their latest hire and that he had been a trainee for approximately six months trying to learn his new job as a teller.

He was kind of a loner. Mary had figured it was because of his being new at the job. Because of his physical size Mary thought he had played some kind of sport like baseball or basketball. He was about six feet six inches tall and had broad shoulders and a relatively narrow waist. Mary had thought Bill handsome in his own way. Buck asked Mary for Bill's home address. After Mary returned with his address, Buck headed out the door of the bank to find Bill.

William Garner lived in a modest second story apartment converted from a nice hacienda-style home. The home had been converted into four small apartments. There was a pool enclosed by a fence in the back for use during the summer months. When Buck got to Bill's apartment, he knocked on the door and waited for the door to open. After a minute he knocked again, this time a little louder; still no answer. He looked in through the window and saw that the apartment had been ransacked inside. Thinking something was amiss, he checked the door to see if it was unlocked, which it was. Buck opened the door and walked in. The ransacked apartment was in pretty bad shape; everything had been moved and turned upside down. The bed had been cut open and the stuffing was all over the floor in the bedroom. The kitchen had the cupboards pulled away from the walls. When Buck walked into the bathroom, lying in the tub was Bill's body. He had taken two bullets to the chest cavity and had bled out in the tub.

Buck called his office and asked for the medical examiner (M.E.) to come to this location. Buck stayed there until the M.E.

showed up. He also called Foster to let him know what was going on. Foster showed up at the same time as the medical examiner, along with Rachael and Evans.

Upon their own inspections of the apartment, Foster and the agents were perplexed.

"Has anything been moved during your investigation?" Evans asked Buck.

"What you see is the same as I found it."

Foster came in after seeing Bill in the bathroom and kind of stood there trying to gather in this new information.

He looked at Buck and shook his head "Now what do we do?"

Buck just stood there. "I'm not sure what to do."

"Do you think this is connected to the robbery?" Rachael asked.

Nobody could answer that question immediately.

After the crime scene had been photographed showing the apartment as it was, Bill's body was taken to the medical examiner's office. As the ambulance left with the body, Buck went over to talk to the medical examiner.

"Do you know the time of death for Bill?" Buck asked.

The medical examiner placed the time of death at about 10:00 pm last night. Almost as a second thought, Buck asked the medical examiner to make sure to get the fingerprints off the body. The medical examiner nodded his head in agreement.

Rachael and Evans canvassed the apartment complex, talking to the next-door neighbors, and as usual, the neighbors heard and saw nothing.

When they all got back to the office everybody was deep in thought, all of them wondering how did Bill fit into this? Maybe it was just a fluke that Bill had been killed, maybe just a coincidence. Or maybe it was something more sinister than they all thought.

Buck spoke first, "What the hell is going on here?"

Nobody answered.

Buck continued, "Three murders and a quarter of a million dollars missing and yet 14,000 dollars is all anybody is saying that was stolen. None of this makes sense at all."

"There must be a connection somehow." Rachael stated.

Evans nodded in agreement. Foster was more than perplexed, he was mad that all they had was only more bodies piling up with no real answers for any of it. Foster walked into the room and sat down. Buck closed his eyes and tried to make sense of all of this new information. His was starting to get a headache. Rachael and Evans were at a loss for words as well.

Rachael spoke first after a long silence. "Maybe we are looking in the wrong direction. Maybe we are looking at this just as a robbery gone bad, and maybe we need to look at it in a different way."

Foster opening his eyes, "Just how do we do that?"

"I'm not sure but maybe this isn't just about the robbery and murders. It could be that there is something else going on and the murders and robbery are a cover-up," Rachael replied.

Buck thought about this for a moment. "You mean we were supposed to find Whitey and Ritchins where we did?"

Evans then spoke up saying, "What do we look for now?"

"Who do we look for now?" Rachael added.

"Let's look at what we got from the top," Rachael stated. "We have a robbery with the bank claiming only 14,000 dollars was stolen, and yet 200,000 is found to have been missing. Then we find the bank has been laundering money for one of the cartels."

"Maybe Whitey and Ritchins were the fall guys for all of this, throwing us off of the trail," Foster added.

"Maybe, just maybe, this was a cover up to something bigger and possibly has been going on all along," Evans replied.

"Just what could be worth a robbery and the murders of four people?" Rachael said, shaking her head.

By now they all knew that they had to start at the beginning with a fresh set of eyes looking at all the information they had gathered from the ground up. Hopefully, they would catch something that would turn the case around.

Buck and Rachael went back to the medical examiner to get the autopsy reports. Evans went back to find the auditor. Foster started looking into the possible witnesses for Bill Garner's murder.

"Let the games begin," Foster said as he was leaving the office.

At this point everybody was tired, hoping that something would give to let them know they were on the right track.

Buck was thinking that he may need to go back out to the desert to look into where they had found the truck and Whitey's body.

"We may need to revisit the places where you found Whitey and the truck," Rachael said.

"Great minds think alike."

Rachael smiled and they continued walking to the medical examiner's office. Once there, the medical examiner confirmed what everybody had known, Mr. Garner had been shot twice in the chest.

"Had there had been a struggle or any-thing out of the ordinary?" Buck asked.

"There was some bruising around the knuckles of the deceased and a contusion on the back of his head. The contusion wasn't enough to knock Mr. Garner out, but it may have been enough to slow him down to the point of being shot by the as-sailant."

"What was the time of death?"

"It took place around 10:00 pm, give or take a half hour."

"What was the caliber of the weapon used?"

"It was a 40 caliber handgun."

"The ballistics showed nothing usable as to the type of ammunition, other than it was a common type sold anywhere," Rachael said.

Buck and Rachael went back to the crime scene and started canvassing the area once again, where they ran into Foster. After spreading out they started asking the neighbors that lived nearby if they had heard any disturbances on the night in question. One of the neighbors thought he had heard a backfire from a car or truck.

"About what time was this?" Rachael asked.

"It was about nine thirty," the neighbor thought.

"Did you see anything unusual around that time?" Buck asked.

"No, I didn't see anything unusual, so I just went back to watching TV."

After another hour of looking around and checking the other neighbors in the area, Rachael and Buck finally headed back to the office. The one thing they both knew was that Mr. Garner died around ten o'clock and that there had been a fight before he had died, thus explaining the shape of the apartment. What amazed both Buck and Rachael is nobody heard the fight while it was going on.

Buck and Rachael waited with Foster for Evans to return so that they could tell Evans what they had learned. When Evans arrived from the auditor's office, you could see on his face that he hadn't learned anything new. As they sat huddled around the table, Buck told the group about the time of death and the caliber of the gun used in the murder. Evans said that the auditor hadn't found anything new or of value in the case. The names associated with the safety-deposit boxes all checked out and nothing was amiss. The background checks for the safety-deposit box holders had yielded nothing out of the ordinary. As far as the auditor was concerned, he was ready to pack up and go back to his office and close everything out.

"What about the safety-deposit box numbered 1001 and the 250, 000 dollar discrepancy from the bank records?" Foster asked.

"That's the only reason the auditor is still here," Evans replied.

Rachael thought for a moment and asked, "I wonder if maybe the safety-deposit box doesn't exist at all."

"With the names of the safety-deposit box owners checking out there is a possibility that maybe the box doesn't exist. The money may have been identified for safety-deposit box 1001 just to keep it away from the regular money in the bank," Evans stated.

Foster thought about this for a moment, "They still need to have had a place for the money to be stored until it could be laundered."

"The safety-deposit box had to be real; it would be too obvious to bank employees with that kind of money hanging around out in the open. I would like to go back and look at the vault where the safety-deposit boxes are kept," Buck interjected.

Did anything of value show up in Mr. Garner's background?" Evans asked.

"Nothing that would raise any flags about the victim," Rachael said.

"Again batting a 1000 for not finding anything worthwhile," Foster said.

At this point Buck asked Rachael if she wanted to take a trip out to the desert to look around. Rachael smirked. "I was wondering when you were going to ask me out on a date."

Buck was embarrassed at first, then laughed at her remark. "Dinner under the stars while looking for clues is very romantic, especially in the desert."

With that, Rachael told Evans that they were going back into the desert to look for more clues.

Evans looked at her. "Good luck, make sure you bring a radio in case something goes wrong."

While Rachael was clearing with Evans, Buck went and got the truck and a few groceries for their trip. He picked Rachael up in front of the sheriff's office.

Rachael looked over at Buck. "Did you bring the food just for yourself, or are you going to share?"

"If you're real nice, I'll share and I won't have to turn this truck around."

Rachael, feigning hurt, said, "Oh please, I'll be nice."

They both laughed at this and started driving out into the desert.

They arrived at the place where Buck had initially found the Ford pickup that Whitey and Ritchins used in their getaway. Rachael got out of Buck's truck to look around and seeing nothing but the

Ford's tracks and where it had bottomed out busting the oil pan, she kept walking with Buck following behind in the truck. As she followed the oil trail, she didn't see it at first, but the second time she looked she realized the truck that had been used by Whitey didn't come from the direction of town. She told Buck, and as he looked at the trail, he saw what Rachael was talking about.

Buck got out of the truck he was driving and caught up to Rachael as she was following the oil trail. As Buck looked at the tracks from the old Ford, he realized that the truck came from the direction of the highway, not from town.

Buck, with a questioning look, said, "Why would they have come from the highway when they should have come directly from New Rio?"

Rachael nodded in agreement, wondering the same thing. After retrieving their truck, Buck and Rachael followed the trail left by the old Ford pickup. After about a mile they realized that the truck had come off of the highway.

Buck muttered to himself out loud, "Why you would leave the highway to take the desert?"

"Maybe they got off the highway because they knew the police would be expecting them to use the highway as a means of escape."

Buck agreed with Rachael's theory. Buck thought maybe they were to meet someone first before their getaway into the desert.

"But who would know about the robbery before it occurred?" Rachael asked.

Buck kept driving the truck another mile and stopped, he got out of the truck and looked on the trail left by the old Ford. Buck called Rachael out to look at the trail. She saw it as well, there was another set of tracks coming from a westerly direction. However, these tracks were from a smaller vehicle, barely recognizable, yet here they were.

"We need to follow these other tracks to see where they come from," Buck said.

Rachael agreed, they got back into the truck and headed west following the trail.

The trail they were following was more like an ATV trail or at least anybody in their right mind wouldn't take a four wheel drive truck on it unless they were desperate. The trail was mainly rock and a lot of sand, they bottomed out a couple times as well. Fortunately, Buck was driving slowly enough to not seriously damage the truck's undercarriage. Even so, Rachael was hanging onto the grips so she wouldn't be tossed around. Buck laughed at her until he bottomed out again the third time. By now Rachael was hanging on for dear life while Buck was trying to control the truck. Neither one of them saw the soft sand with a rock sticking out of the side of it. Buck drove right over the rock with his front tire and they both heard the sound of air escaping from the tire. They looked at each other and stared. What do we do now?

Buck looked at her. "You wanted a second date with a wild and crazy guy, well, you got it."

She looked at him. "A wild and crazy guy, not a wild and crazy driver."

They got out of the truck and looked at the tire. The tire had a two inch cut along the sidewall. Nothing could fix this tire, except replacing it altogether. Buck crawled under the tailgate of the truck looking for the spare. Much to his surprise, it was flat as well, and to make things worse, he couldn't budge it to get at it even if he had wanted to. The truck had bottomed out in the back as well. Buck looked around to see if he could find something to wedge the truck to raise the back end. Looking around the area for about five minutes, he could find nothing.

When Buck got back to the truck, Rachael had all of the food laid out on the tailgate.

She looked at Buck. "Would you like your bologna sandwich under glass or do you prefer sand with your mustard?"

"Where are the candles?"

Rachael laughed at this and poured some water into a cup.

After drinking some water Rachael asked, "What do we do now, where do we go?"

Buck thought about this for a moment as he ate his sandwich and knelt down to draw in the sand.

"Here is where I think we are, and here is where New Rio is," putting a large X in the sand.

"How far is it from New Rio?"

"A day's journey if we follow the trail we found."

"I tried the radio I brought with me, but couldn't raise anybody."

"Must be in a dead zone; we need to get to the top of one of these mountains and try the radio again."

With that, Buck looked into the sky. "It's too late to start out for New Rio tonight; no need to break our legs on the rocks, especially the ones we don't see because it's dark."

"You really know how to show a girl a good time."

Buck laughed and prepared a place for them to sleep. The evening chill came on as the sun went down and the fire was just starting to get them warm. As they huddled together to stay warm Rachael put her head on Bucks shoulder and started to doze a little.

"This is one date I'm not going to easily forget," She said.

Buck held her close and chuckled and kissed her on the forehead.

Rachael reached up and kissed him as well. "Good night."

The next morning when the sun arose at about 5:00 am, they both were wrapped in a blanket that Buck had used earlier when he was by himself. Buck looked at Rachael in the early morning glow of the sunlight and couldn't help but notice how beautiful she was in the morning.

"Good morning, beautiful," Buck said as he handed her a bologna sandwich for breakfast.

Rachael looked at him. "Why, aren't you the gentleman for having breakfast sent up to our room."

Buck looked at her and laughed. He reached out to her and kissed her, she responded by returning his kiss. After their embrace Buck looked around to see if there was anything he had missed from the night before. As nothing had changed, he grabbed the blanket, fashioning a backpack out of it, then put in the jug of water and food. When it was all done, he put it on his back and asked Rachael, "Are you ready to head out?"

"We need to leave a note for room service to have the truck made up for later," Rachael replied.

Buck smiled, took her hand and started walking towards the mountains in the direction of New Rio.

# Chapter VIII

Foster had made his way to the bank and was looking for the safety-deposit boxes hoping he would find where box 1001 was hiding. From the looks of it nothing was out of place. Foster kept trying to figure out what had happened to the box. He had looked into the vault where the safety-deposit boxes were lined up along the one side of the vault. The other side of the vault had a small safe where the money was kept overnight when the bank was closed. The safe itself had been there since the bank opened years earlier. Foster thought to himself that they probably hadn't changed the combination on the inside safe since it was put in. The safe stuck out maybe a foot from the wall. Foster thought this unusual seeing as how the safe was made to fit the vault.

He went back into the main portion of the bank and talked to the loan officer. "Have there been any modifications done to the vault since it was put in?"

"This is the original vault and the safe was put in years later after the bank started getting more deposits."

"Do you know when this occurred?"

"They put the safe in about a year ago."

Foster went back to the vault to look more closely at the safe. This didn't make any sense at all. The safe was as old as the vault, yet had only been put in a year earlier. Foster, stepping out of the vault, called Evans to meet him at the bank. Fifteen minutes later Evans showed up. Foster explained about the safe inside the vault and the age difference for it. Evans motioned for them to go into the bank vault. This time the loan officer went with Foster and Evans into the vault. Not sure as to why she did but more out of curiosity she kept quiet while Foster explained again to Evans about the interior safe. When they had finished talking to each, other Foster looked at the loan officer and asked her to restate what she had told him earlier.

"The safe was put in about a year ago, when the deposits started getting bigger."

"How much had the deposits increased to require a safe?"

"When all of the banks start having half a million dollars on a regular basis, more security was required for insurance purposes."

When Evans heard this, he headed out of the vault with Foster following. Evans started asking around for the auditor. Foster caught on quickly as to what Evans was doing; if anybody would have information about the money it would be the auditor.

It was noon when Buck and Rachael were able to get to the top of a mountain to try the radio again. All in all, they figured they had traveled half the distance to New Rio. The trail was good for walking and nothing seemed to impair their hike. The radio came to life when Rachael called out, the sheriff's department answered her call and, feeling a wave of relief, Buck gave their approximate position so that they could send someone to come get them. At this point they sat down to catch their breath, waiting to see if they needed to give better directions as to where they were in reference to the rescuers. After about 30 minutes they saw a trail of dust coming towards them. They radioed the sheriff's office to verify that they had sent someone out to meet them. Once this was confirmed by the sheriff's office, another voice came on and asked for better directions to get to where Buck and Rachael were. Buck reminded the rescuers that they needed a tire for the truck they had left behind. The radio crackled again saying they had one with them.

Pretty soon an ATV side-by-side with what looked like a donut on the back of it was coming up the trail that Buck and Rachael were on. The driver of the ATV was happy to see them and offered to take them back down to the truck. Buck and Rachael quickly obliged and when back on the trail they went to find the truck. When they got to the truck, Buck quickly changed the tire and with the help of the ATV was able to pull the truck out of the sand. At this point Buck and Rachael rode back together in the truck, backtracking to where the trail they had been following merged with the known trail. The ATV followed a distance away to avoid eating the dust from the truck. When they got back into New Rio, Buck dropped Rachael off at her motel room to get cleaned up. Buck headed to his own place to do the same.

Foster and Evans were back in the office when Buck and Rachael showed up. One look at them both and you could tell from the sunburns that it had been no picnic for either of them being out in the desert. Once all of the kidding died down and things were back to normal, both had information to share.

Buck went first. "We followed an ATV trail that split off from the main trail the getaway vehicle had taken and found that it led back into town."

"It looked as if Whitey and Ritchins met someone out there in the desert before getting stuck in the old Ford," Rachael stated.

Foster and Evans were not surprised by this new information, much to the dismay of Buck and Rachael.

Evans spoke next. "I think we know where safety-deposit box 1001 is."

Foster jumped in at this point saying, "It's in the bank vault somewhere."

This news had Buck and Rachael all excited.

"How did you figure this out?"

"That old safe in the vault was as old as the vault itself, but had only been put in the year before. We need a warrant to go look for it."

"We're waiting for the judge to sign off on it," Evans said.

With this new information about the ATV trail and the old safe in the vault, they all agreed that whoever had planned the robbery and murders was still around town and patiently waiting for the trail to go cold to start up again.

Evans made a suggestion of contacting the DEA (Drug Enforcement Agency) about the drug trail coming and going out of New Rio. "They may have some information we're not aware of."

"What have we got to lose? They may have an idea as to who we should be looking for," Foster said.

Buck thought to himself, what was the common denominator in this case? Was it the bank, people in the bank, the syndicate and maybe the drugs, or could it be all of the above? He didn't know where to start with all of it.

So he asked Rachael, "Would you like to go to dinner and maybe discuss the case?"

"I'm famished and as long as you're buying I'm ready to go."

"How about a bologna sandwich with some fries?" Buck said.

She rolled her eyes and laughed.

While waiting for their order to come up at the café, Buck asked Rachael, "So what's your take on all of this?"

She put her hot cocoa down and looked at it for minute, "It's obvious that whoever has planned this is still in the area. It's pretty ingenious how this has all been carried out so far. There has to be more money involved than what's been taken; just how much remains to be seen."

Buck nodded his head in agreement. By then the food arrived and they started eating. Not much was said as they ate their food. They both seemed lost in their own thoughts about the case.

Finally Rachael said, "Maybe we need to look at the trail of money from Chicago and where it goes from there."

Buck put down his fork. "Just how do we do that?"

"Let's go ask Ritchins to see if he has any suggestions that will help. Maybe, just maybe, he knows more than we think."

"Let's do it tomorrow; I'm bushed tonight," Buck agreed.

"You must be getting old, can't keep up with the kids anymore."

"You may be right. Staying out all night howling at the moon and climbing a mountain isn't as easy as it used to be."

Rachael heartily agreed.

Buck dropped Rachael off at her room and headed back to his place. When he opened the door, he was shocked to see it all torn apart. The mattress from his bed was ripped open and lying in the front room; the drawers were pulled completely out and lying on the floor. The front room furniture was tossed about as if a tornado had cut a path to the kitchen. Broken dishes were lying on the counter and on the floor. Every step he took he could feel glass crunching under his feet. Buck placed a phone call to Foster.

"I need a place to stay tonight; do you have an extra bed in your room?"

"Why?"

"I'm having my house gone through to update the interior. I'll explain more when I get there."

The following morning Buck and Foster showed up at Buck's place to look at the mess left behind.

"We must be getting close to the answers were looking for," Foster said.

"Now for the fun part, cleaning it up."

"Do you need any help?"

"No, I got this."

At that, Foster went into work and left Buck to clean up his house.

Foster told Rachael and Evans about what had transpired at Buck's place.

"Is Buck okay?" Rachael asked.

"Yeah, just surprised and concerned by what he had found in his house."

"I wonder if we may be next," Evans said.

"I wonder what they hoped to find at Buck's place?" Rachael added.

"That's the question of the day," Foster replied.

Evans heard the phone ring and picked it up. After about 30 seconds he said thanks for the update and hung up. Both Foster and Rachael were looking at him, waiting to hear what he had learned from the call.

"The call was from the DEA office in Phoenix. They claimed that they had no inputs from their side of the fence. I personally think that the cartels are involved with this somehow," Evans said.

"We need to find the drop-off point for the drugs coming in and the money going out," Rachael said.

"You've been reading my mind again," Evans exclaimed.

Rachael smiled and nodded at the comment.

Buck came walking in about two hours later as everyone was looking at the map of Arizona. On the map were highlighted areas of Phoenix, New Rio and the small Mexican town across the border where they had found Ritchins. All of it looked like a puzzle with big pieces being fit into the square frame.

Buck came over and asked, "What are you looking for?"

"We're trying to find a connection between the areas on the map." Evans replied.

Buck looked at the map for a minute, "With everything pointing back to New Rio, especially the redecorating of my place, Bill's murder, and his place being ransacked, I think this is a local job." With that thought in mind he asked, "What is the travel route that Jim takes for his job?"

Foster ran over to his desk and rummaged through the papers looking for

Jim's interview file. Once he found it he brought it back to the group and laid it out next to the map.

"Jim never really gave us the information about his route; he just stated that he would go into Phoenix on a weekly basis."

"We need to follow him next time he goes out on one of his trips," Buck said.

Rachael said, "Shotgun!" and smiled.

Everybody grinned at the comment. Buck turned a little red in the face and smiled as well.

Evans spoke up, "Have we done an extensive background check on Jim?"

"Jim doesn't strike me as being the ringleader in this setup. There has to be someone else with lots of power for this big of an operation," Foster replied.

"But who could it be and where are they located?" Rachael asked.

Foster nodded. "Who wants to take the first shift of the stakeout?"

"Buck and I will take the first shift. Could you guys relieve us about midnight?" Rachael asked.

"Evans and I will be there for the second shift," Foster said.

The first shift was pretty easy, no outward signs or activity other than the typical stuff.

Jim picked up his son from a neighbor who had been watching him and then headed home for dinner. They could see through the window that after dinner Jim and his son were watching a little television before heading off to sleep. This occurred around 10:00 pm.

Rachael and Buck were sitting far enough away in the truck that they were able to see the entire area without being seen themselves. They had parked about a half mile away with some other cars from the impound lot nearby. Rachael was in the passenger side of the truck with Buck at the wheel. Rachael would get out every once in a while in order to stretch her legs and Buck would do the same as well. They both had binoculars and every once in a while they would check the cars coming by as they approached Jim's house. At about 11:30 they saw a black Cadillac SUV drive by twice. Rachael wasn't able to get the license plate of the SUV because of the angle that they were driving. The fancy SUV stayed only for a moment outside the house, then would take off down the street. Buck walked down towards Jim's house to try and get a better look at what was going on with the black Cadillac. Unfortunately, the vehicle never came back after the second time. Buck came back to the truck, got back in and tried to warm up a little bit to shake the cold off. Rachael put her arms around him to help warm him up. About thirty minutes past midnight Foster and Evans showed up and took over the stakeout. Buck told Foster about the black Cadillac SUV coming around twice during their watch.

"We'll keep an eye out for it," Foster said.

With that, Buck and Rachael headed home.

"Buck, are you ready to go to sleep yet?" Rachael asked.

"No, what are you thinking?"

"I was wondering if there were places open this late for breakfast."

"There's a truck stop on the highway that's open 24 hours. That being said, it's about 30 minutes from here, or would you prefer my place?"

"You have any dishes left that aren't broken?" Rachael grinned.

"I have some paper plates and plastic forks to use," Buck laughed.

Rachael couldn't help smiling, "Why, Buck, you think of everything don't you?"

"I was once a boy scout and I'm always prepared."

And with that, they headed to Buck's place for breakfast. The next day found Foster and Evans tired and half asleep from their time at the stakeout. Foster called Buck and Rachael and told them to meet at the stakeout place.

When Buck and Rachael arrived at where Evans and Foster were staked out, Evans said, "Are you guys ready for a road trip?"

"We watched Jim getting ready for the day and saw that he was loading his car up for another road trip. This occurred around 8:00 this morning," Foster said.

Buck looked at Rachael and they both said, "Yes."

"Jim dropped his son off at the neighbor's house next door and was putting the final touches for his trip together," Foster stated.

Buck and Rachael were ready for the road trip after filling the truck up with gas and getting some stuff to eat along the way.

Foster and Evans followed Jim to the highway and radioed for Buck and Rachael to meet them at the truck stop where Jim had stopped to fill up with gas. Buck and Rachael took over from there and waited for Jim to get on the high- way. At this point Evans and Foster went back home to get some sleep.

Buck positioned his truck behind one of the eighteen wheelers in the sleeping area at the stop. Buck and Rachael said nothing to each other while they waited for Jim to pay for the gas. Jim came out of the truck stop and got into his car and headed west on the highway, taking the on ramp heading to Phoenix. Buck and Rachael were about two car lengths behind Jim when they got on the on ramp. Buck was sure that with the morning traffic heading into the city Jim would think that they were just going to work. Jim kept going in the direction of Phoenix and Buck and Rachael were following about half a mile behind. Jim took the turnoff for the 101 exit, which put him on the loop that circled the city proper. He then took the 67th Avenue exit and headed north past the construction area around Thunderbird Park. There he turned right on Paradise Road and drove to a junk-yard that specialized in foreign cars. He was met by a guy who looked like he was suffering from some kind of cancer in the belly. The guy wasn't wearing a shirt and you could see the sores on his belly. Buck and Rachael pulled to the side of the road and watched. In a few minutes Jim came out of the trailer that was located at the junkyard with a gym bag and after loading it into his car took off and headed west towards the highway.

Rachael had taken photos of Jim's exchange with the guy at the junkyard. Jim had handed over a small briefcase in exchange for the gym bag. The briefcase was too small for anything other than money. However, both Buck and Rachael surmised that the gym bag had drugs in it, especially the way Jim had to use both hands to lift it into the trunk of the car.

Buck and Rachael continued to follow Jim from a safe distance, watching Jim's car as he made his way past the high school and headed towards the highway. By now two other vehicles had showed up, both of them kind of fancy. Buck wondered what this meant for them as far as trying to tail Jim's car.

"Don't worry, I've seen this before. The two cars are an escort for Jim; one will take the lead and the other will follow Jim," Rachael said.

Buck looked at Rachael questioningly as she continued to take pictures of the two cars and the occupants inside the escort cars.

Rachael replied to the look, "This is standard practice for hauling drugs from place to place. This way it keeps everybody honest and safe in case Jim gets pulled over by the troopers for some unknown reason or hijacked by the competition."

Buck nodded as he continued following Jim. Then one of the escort cars took the lead and the other escort car followed Jim closely until they reached the highway. Once on the highway the trailing car followed about a quarter mile behind Jim. Buck had to keep his truck behind the trailing car without arousing any suspicion.

When they got into Phoenix the two cars and Jim took the 75th Avenue turnoff and headed into the business section of the area behind the mall. Buck continued following the cars as they made their way behind the mall. Buck and Rachael got out of the truck and walked as if they were going into the mall. Once there they split up to follow Jim and the drivers of the pace cars, hoping it would lead to the pickup or drop- off point for the drugs.

The mall was a two-story mall, quite large and usually crowded; however, this early in the afternoon the shopping crowds were just starting to show. Rachael took the upper floor and Buck tailed them on the first floor. Buck watched Jim go into the ice cream store in the food court. Jim was carrying the gym bag full of the money or drugs. All Buck could do at this point was wait and see what happened next. After five minutes Jim came out from behind the ice cream counter with a different gym bag filled with something in it. You could tell that this gym bag seemed heavier than the bag he had when he walked in. Buck figured it must have been money inside this bag. Jim proceeded to the door of the mall he had walked in from the outside. He met his escorts on the way through the food court, and they walked out to their cars as if they had been shopping. By this time Rachael and Buck met each other in the food court and followed Jim outside to their truck.

Jim was already in his car and had started out of the mall parking lot to get on 75th Avenue and was headed north towards the 101 loop. Buck followed closely this time, not worried about being spotted as there were enough cars around to not arouse suspicion. Rachael got the license plates of both the lead and tail cars that had escorted Jim to the mall. Jim took the 101 loop turnoff and headed south to the interstate. The pace cars with Jim took their positions as they had when coming into the city. Buck and Rachael continued following Jim as he headed west on the interstate towards California. Rachael used her cell phone and called the FBI office she was assigned to in Phoenix and asked for information about the license plate numbers. About three minutes later her cell phone rang and gave her the information about the license plates she had requested.

The two pace cars belonged to Oliver Martinez and Raul Hernandez. Both were connected to the mafia based in the Phoenix chapter and were known to be drug pushers and enforcers for the local drug cartel. At this time they were involved with money laundering throughout the state. They had been suspects in murders for hire, though it had never been proved. Rachael, upon hearing this, told Buck what she had learned. Buck mulled this over in his head trying to decide on how to handle this new information. Rachael was still on her cell phone waiting for Buck to say something.

"So how do you want to handle this?" Rachael asked.

"Let's see how this plays out."

At that, Rachael terminated her call and sat back and waited to see what would happen next.

Buck and Rachael followed Jim's caravan of cars all the way to the California state line. They then had to turn back because Buck had no jurisdiction in California. Stopping at a truck stop to get some lunch, they hadn't said much all the way back till now.

Rachael spoke first. "What do you make of this?"

Buck shook his head. "I'm not sure what to make of it." Buck continued to eat his hamburger and fries, "I think this is bigger than we thought from the beginning. I think Jim is a gopher for the drug cartels, helps launder the money and move the drugs across Arizona and California."

"Who do you think Jim is working for?"

"That is the 64,000 dollar question here."

Upon finishing their lunch Buck and Rachael headed out to their truck. While getting in they heard some commotion coming from the front of the gas pumps. Looking in that direction, they both recognized one of the pace cars that followed Jim sitting at one of the gas pumps. The driver was trying to put gas in his car and wasn't having any luck with it. Buck started towards the pumps and told Rachael to back him up. She instinctively drew her weapon and held it by her side, watching him close the gap between him and the pace car. Buck was watching the driver fumbling around by the side of his car. He could tell the driver was in some kind of pain, and then he noticed the stain in the guy's shirt. Buck could tell that it was a bullet wound in the man's abdomen. The blood had run down and stained the drivers pant leg. Buck rushed over to the driver and helped him lie down next to his car.

"Rachael, call 911 for an ambulance!" Buck called out.

Rachael came over after making the call. "Is he going to make it?"

Buck looked up and shook his head no.

"He's lost too much blood."

A couple of minutes later the ambulance drove up with a State Highway Patrol officer following close by. At this point Buck and Rachael walked away from the scene and let the medics do what they could for the driver. The trooper started asking questions to the bystanders nearby. Buck thought it best not to say anything at this time about their business and got into their truck and drove off. Rachael identified the driver as Oliver Martinez, who had been driving the lead pace car. They both wondered what had happened to Martinez after they had crossed the state line.

Rachael called her office again and asked to speak to the lead agent in charge. When he answered the phone, she asked, "Has anything occurred within the last hour in and around the California-Arizona state line?"

"Negative, I'll keep checking."

Rachael closed her cell phone and put it down on the dashboard of the truck.

Buck looked at her for a moment. "We need to get back to our office." With that they kept driving.

When Buck and Rachael got into the office later that afternoon, they were the only ones around. Foster and Evans were out of the office at their respective hotel rooms.

"We need to let them know what happened on our trip," Buck said.

"I'm not quite sure how to tell them about all of this."

"It will wait till tomorrow."

With that he dropped her off at her hotel room and went home. Buck walked into his place and found the couch and laid down on it and was out. Rachael decided to take a shower and clean off some of the grime from the traveling. The water felt good on her back as she leaned up against the shower stall. As she was relaxing, her cell phone rang. Upon hearing it she stepped out of the shower, wrapped a towel around herself and answered the phone. The voice on the other end identified himself as her boss.

"Since your last contact an incident was reported by the local police dealing with a body found on the California side of the border. It looks like a gang-style murder."

"How many bodies were found?"

"Only one and he was driving one of the cars you called in an inquiry on."

"Did they find anything else at the scene?"

"Negative, the only things found at the scene were the car and one Raul Hernandez, who had been shot in the back of the head."

Rachael was surprised by this. "Were there any drugs or money found?"

"No, nothing was found, just the car and Hernandez."

Rachael closed out the call with the typical pleasantries and hung up her phone. At this point Rachael got back into the shower and finished it off with putting her head under the shower nozzle for a couple of seconds, turned off the water and crawled into her bed and was fast asleep.

# CHAPTER IX

The next day everybody was there for the brief, and all were waiting to tell their portion of the story.

Foster started off by saying, "Jim never came back after he was tracked to California."

"We finally received a warrant to search Jim's house and found no evidence tying him to the bank robbery or the murders. However, we did find a receipt for a storage rental in his desk. We went down to the storage facility and got a key from the proprietor to look around inside. We found drug paraphernalia and money wrappers stacked in one of the corners of the unit, with a money-counting machine next to it. Inside one of the other lockers on the other side of the unit we found money and a couple of semi-autos with boxes of shells," Evans interjected.

"I talked to the proprietor about the rental unit, and he said that the unit had been rented for quite some time, about a year or so. The renter always paid in cash, six months at a time," Foster said.

"The crime lab checked for fingerprints and found Jim's prints everywhere inside. And we are still waiting on the ballistics checks for the semi-autos to see if they linked up with any criminal activity in the data base," Evans said.

Now it was Buck and Rachael's turn to tell of their adventure following Jim to California.

"Buck and I followed Jim to the California border as he left from a Phoenix mall, where he dropped off what we think was money and picked up a bag of what we think was drugs," Rachael said.

At that point Buck interjected, "While we were having lunch at the truck stop, we witnessed one of the pace cars pull alongside the gas pump and watched the driver get out and fall to the ground and die from being shot."

Both Evans and Foster sat there totally shocked by what Rachael and Buck told them.

Rachael followed up by saying, "Our boss at the FBI office called to let me know there was a report of a murder in California."

At this, Buck looked up. "Were they able to identify the body?"

"Yes, it was the second driver with Jim."

"What about Jim?" Foster asked.

At this, Rachael shook her head. "Nobody knows what happened to Jim. He may have killed both drivers for the drugs, or he may have been killed himself."

Evans at this point asked, "Do we still stake out Jim's place; maybe he won't be back?"

While everybody was thinking about Evan's questions the phone rang interrupting their thoughts. It was the auditor calling for Evans.

Evans answered the phone. "Hello," paused for a moment and said he would meet the auditor in about five minutes.

As Evans hung up the phone, he looked at Foster. "Good news, the auditor found something useful."

All of them got up to go see what the auditor had found.

When the team showed up at the bank, the auditor was surprised to see all of them there. He took a deep breath and started talking. "Glad all of you could make it."

He directed them towards the safe vault with the loan officer in tow.

Once everybody was inside the vault the auditor started off by saying, "Special Agent Evans got me to thinking about the layout of the old safe inside the vault." The auditor patted on the top of the safe and opened the door. "As you can see, the safe sits out from the wall by at least a foot or more, which made me want to look inside the safe."

With the safe door opened, the loan officer pulled out one of the safety-deposit boxes off the top shelf.

The auditor spoke, "Look at the size of the safety-deposit box in relation to the size of the safe."

By now everybody was looking at the size of the box versus the size of the safe. All of a sudden everybody saw it and the lights came on inside their heads. The safety-deposit box was half the size of the safe interior. At this point the auditor reached in and pulled out another box that was behind the safety-deposit box that was already out.

With this new box being held by the auditor, Buck asked, "Pray tell, is that box 1001?"

With a grin of a Cheshire cat on his face, the auditor said, "Yes," and at that point opened the box.

Inside the box were neat stacks of money, all in all about 100 thousand dollars. When that sank, in the auditor pulled out another regular safety-deposit box and handed it to the loan officer. Then reaching in again, pulled another box from behind the second box. With this, he opened the second box and, again, inside was neatly stacked money which equaled another 100 thousand dollars. By now everybody was excited about the new find.

"Are there any more behind the others?" Foster asked.

"Yes, behind every one of the regular boxes there are more; however, that being said, these two were the only ones with money in the," the auditor replied.

Evans looked at the loan officer and asked, "Who had access to the safe?"

"The head teller and I were the only ones who had access to this safe besides the owners of the regular safety-deposit boxes. They would have to go through me or the head teller to get inside their box."

"Let me guess who the head teller is!" Foster said.

Everybody knew the answer before the name came up; it had been Karen Olds.

"Hell of a price to pay for 200 thousand dollars. I hope she thought it was worth it," Buck said.

"Somebody did," replied Foster.

After talking to the auditor for another couple of minutes, he promised them that a report would be filed in the next couple of days from there they would need the FBI to come in and retain the money for evidence.

The auditor had also stated, "None of the money was ever registered in any account; the money was sitting in the fake safety-deposit boxes for who knows how long. The tally books for the drug money have not been found as of yet."

"I wonder if they may be in Jim's place or maybe in William's place," Rachael said.

"It could be the reason that he is dead. It could be Bill found the tally book and tried to use it to blackmail Jim," Foster added.

"We need to go back and look at both places again, this time with a fine tooth comb," Evans said.

"Rachael and I will go to Bill's place, while you two go to Jim's place," Buck said.

And with that, they headed out of the bank to their destinations.

When Buck and Rachael got to Bill's place, they noticed the door was slightly ajar. Drawing their guns and waiting to the count of three they opened the door wider to look inside. Once inside they went from room to room clearing the apartment. The place had been ransacked; everything that could be upended was.

Buck looked around as Rachael came from the back area. "Looks like someone beat us here."

Rachael nodded in agreement. With that they conducted their own ransacking of the apartment. As Rachael continued going over the apartment, Buck went to the neighbors and asked if anybody had heard or seen anything. By the time Buck got back Rachael was done going through the apartment. Neither of them had any luck finding any new information dealing with the drugs or the money found in the bank.

As Buck stood there looking at the mess of the apartment, he thought to himself, "Where would I hide a ledger for transactions and money laundering?" Buck scanned the living room and his eyes settled on one of the air vents in the ceiling. He then got a step ladder and went over to the one vent that was in the living room. Buck climbed the step ladder to the top step and with a screwdriver undid the vent cover and with his flashlight peered into the opening of the vent.

Rachael, watching this entire exercise, heard Buck say, "I think I found something."

Buck reached in and pulled a small wrapped package out of the vent carefully handing the bundle to Rachael. Stepping down from the step ladder and watching Rachael carefully unwrap the wrapping from around the package, Buck and Rachael were anxious to see what was inside. Once fully separated from the wrapping, both could see that it contained a box about three inches by three inches with a lid on it. Removing the lid they found a key and a note. Buck held onto the key while Rachael looked over the note.

As Rachael read the note, she said, "It looks as if it's some kind of code or riddle."

Rachael handed the note to Buck to let him read it as well. After looking at the writing on the paper, Buck leaned up against the wall next to the doorway. Buck let out a couple of cuss words, which caught Rachael off guard. Rachael was looking at Buck surprised.

After a moment of silence Buck politely apologized to Rachael for the outburst and exclaimed, "When are we going to get a break in this case? We have more bodies than we can count and still no real direction to go."

Rachael understood how he felt. "I agree, this is really frustrating to have all of this going on and not knowing where to look next."

Rachael waved the piece of paper in her hand. "But cheer up; we have a new clue with a riddle to solve."

Buck smiled at this. "Well, we did find this, didn't we?"

Smiling now, Buck continued, "All we need to do now is find out where the key fits."

"Maybe the clue to the location is in this note."

After looking at the note Rachael read it aloud. "<u>The big wheels sometimes go round and round and yet always come home.</u>"

Buck listened to her as she read the note, more perplexed now than ever, he threw his hands in the air and said, "Oh boy, now where do we look for big wheels that always come home? What are they, boomerang tires?"

Rachael was feeling the same way as well, but this time she said, "Let's go get something to eat and worry about this later."

Buck agreed with her, smiling, and with that they headed to the local café in town.

As they sat eating their lunch, Evans and Foster walked in. Buck, seeing them first, waved at them to let them know where they were. Evans and Foster made their way over to the booth and sat down opposite them. Once seated the waitress came over and took their orders. When she left with their orders, Evans asked, "Did you find anything worth looking for?"

Rachael told them that Bill's place had been ransacked and that they had found a box inside the vent with a key and a note with a riddle on it. Both Foster and Evans were impressed that they had found anything at all, considering the condition of Bill's place.

"Aw shucks, twern't nothing sirs, just doing our job," Rachael said.

Foster and Evans chuckled over her statement and even Buck smiled.

With that Buck asked Foster and Evans, "Did you find anything at Jim's place?"

Foster spoke first, "Jim's place had been ransacked as well. We were unable to find anything that would help us find some answers."

"Whoever it was that had done the searching of these two places most likely didn't find what they were looking for. This can only mean that Jim is still out there and on the run from the people who ransacked his place," Evans added.

The food order for both Foster and Evans appeared at the table. Foster took a bite of his food and Evans salted his fries before taking a bite. As they sat there, Rachael read the riddle to Foster and Evans. A look of perplexity was on their faces as they tried to make sense of the riddle.

Evans spoke, "What the hell kind of clue is that?"

"Reminds me of the children's song about the wheels on the bus go round and round," Foster added.

Rachael closed her eyes for a second and started to hum the tune.

Buck looked at her and laughed. "You should never quit your day job."

Rachael feigned being hurt and laughed at herself for humming the song. "It's a catchy song."

Evans looked at Rachael, smiling. "The things you learn about your partner while on assignment."

Having the key and the riddle to solve was now the top priority of the team. They figured Jim was either dead or had gone underground to avoid capture. Not only was the government looking for him, but the mafia was looking for him as well because they had been ripped off of their drugs/money and had two of their people killed.

Evans and Buck took the key down to a local locksmith to try and identify the type of key it was and where it would be used. Buck knew the locksmith on a first-name basis only. As the conversation unfolded, the locksmith identified the key as fitting some kind of locker you would find in a bowling alley, bus stop, or maybe a home-made safe. The only problem with this new information was that there wasn't a bus stop or bowling alley in New Rio. The closest bus stop was in Tucson, as was the bowling alley. Finding a homemade safe was the safest bet they had to go on. The only question is where to look for it. It could be buried in Jim's or Bill's backyard or up on a mountain or lord knows where. The screws just keep turning on this case.

When Buck and Evans returned to the sheriff's office, they told Foster and

Rachael what they had learned. You could tell that after hearing the news everybody was feeling down. They had another set of clues that weren't really good clues. By now everyone was sitting around wondering what to do next.

Buck was getting upset. "I need to get some fresh air out in the desert."

Rachael, upon hearing this decided to go with him by gently asking, "Could I go with you?"

Buck nodded in the affirmative and off they went.

"Evans and I will stay close to the office in case something like a new clue came up," Foster said halfway laughing.

Buck and Rachael got into the truck and headed out into the desert. By now it was getting towards evening, which meant it was getting cooler and clearer with the stars starting to show in the night sky. Buck went to his favorite place out in the desert called Huff's Peak. The road out there was clear and easy to follow. It led to a ridge where you could sit and watch the town lights come on one at a time. Up here it was cool and the air refreshing. Buck had this one place where you could sit comfortably with your legs over the edge and your back up against the rocks. When Rachael and Buck got to his favorite place to sit, Rachael stood there a moment taking it all in. The desert valley below her and the stars shining in the night sky were breathtaking. From where they sat, the stars went on forever and touched the desert floor off in the distance. As Rachael was admiring the view, Buck was deep in thought. After a short time, Rachael sat down next to Buck. All was quiet.

Buck was the first to speak, breaking the silence. "When things got bad at our house, I would come out and sit here until I could clear my head."

Rachael sat and listened without saying anything. She too was caught up in the case. As she listened to Buck sort things out about the case, she continued to sit and gaze out into the desert. She took hold of Buck's hand and held it. It was her way of letting him know that she was there for and with him. Rachael looked up into the sky and saw the Milky Way, like a thin veil, as it stretched across the sky. Living in Phoenix, the lights of the city would have blocked the Milky Way from view. Pretty soon Buck put his arm around Rachael and kissed her as he held her next to him. Rachael in turn kissed him as well, snuggling up next to him. Buck wondered if she would consider staying here with him forever as his wife.

With that, he turned to her and said, "I love you."

Rachael looked at him not saying anything, and kissed him again. For the first time in her life she felt at peace with the world and all of the craziness of the case. They sat there for two more hours just sitting and enjoying each other's company. About midnight they decided to head on down the mountain. With the moon and the city lights shining they found their way home to New Rio, where Buck dropped Rachael off at her place, and from there Buck headed home to his place.

The next morning everybody seemed to be in better spirits. Everyone had gathered around the conference table with Foster up at the whiteboard, a black marker in his hand. Foster had drawn a vertical line separating the board down the middle. On one side of the line he wrote "known" and on the other side he wrote "unknown". With that they started listing all of the knowns.

Buck started off. "Bodies identified and robbery."

Foster wrote the names down.

Then Rachael offered, "Mafia and Jim are dead or on the run."

"The money in the bank's safety-deposit box and Chicago and money laundering," Evans said.

At this, Foster said, looking at the board, "Is there any common denominator in any of this?"

With this question there was a pause.

"Let's look at the unknown," Foster said.

Again, Buck started off. "Jim, alive or dead?"

"The key, where does it go?" Rachael added.

Evans followed suit by adding, "The syndicates."

Foster quickly wrote the unknowns down on the whiteboard. Again, Foster asked the question that he had asked earlier; however, this time he added Ritchins' name plus the others who had wound up dead onto the unknown side.

When Foster was finished, he stood back and surveyed the writing on the whiteboard. Evans saw that there may have been a connection between the syndicates with the drugs and money laundering.

"The murder of the tellers from the bank," added Buck.

Rachael thought about what she was looking at. "Maybe a drug deal gone bad. Maybe an agreement that took place between the syndicates went bad for at least one of the enterprises."

With this question Evans thought out loud, "It could be one of the players got greedy, and maybe they were cutting their losses by taking out the players involved."

"Who stood to lose the most out of this partnership?" Foster asked.

"Both of them; greed overrode their own lack of trust for each other," Buck stated.

Foster at this juncture said, "Maybe Whitey was sent down here to clean up a mess and got killed for his troubles. Maybe Jim was supposed to pick up where Whitey left off."

By now a scenario started forming in everyone's mind.

"Jim killed the mafia guys to get even for his syndicate bosses being ripped off by taking the drugs and the money on the way out of town. It could be Jim is alive and well back in Chicago, living it up with the mafia's money and drugs, knowing that the mafia wouldn't dare to try and get their stuff back from the syndicate. One thing for sure, someone got caught holding the bag and someone had to pay for it," Foster said.

Evans spoke up next, "Why don't we put a BOLO out on Jim in the Chicago area and see what comes up."

Rachael agreed with this and added, "Maybe we need to run a check on the two drivers for the Mafia as well."

"Do you think the FBI could assist us with the safe key?" Buck asked.

"We got nothing to lose and everything to gain by asking," Evans commented.

Foster was still looking at the whiteboard and pondering if there was anything local that would help in solving the case.

Foster looked towards them asking, "The mafia is located in Phoenix, aren't they?"

Everybody nodded in agreement, "Then why are they operating way out here? It seems to me that there could be a territorial dispute with someone else's group. Maybe, just maybe, there is a third party involved in this."

Buck asked at this point, "Where do we look for that third party?"

"Do you guys work confidential informants?" Rachael asked.

Buck smiled at this, "The only confidential informants we have go to the beauty salon every Tuesday at three."

They all laughed at this.

"There is a possibility that some of the low life's in town might know about something going down that we may have overlooked," Buck continued.

With that they started thinking of whom the third party might be and what would they have to gain from all of this.

Buck asked Rachael if she wanted to meet some of New Rio's finest citizenry, to which she replied, "Why I thought you would never ask."

Evans headed out to call the main FBI office in Phoenix to find out more about the Mafia. Foster sat there thinking for a moment, then got up saying that his money was still on Jim. With this he wanted to make sure Jim was dead and if not, where to start looking for him. He went to check his resources regarding the shooting of the two mafia drivers.

As with all towns, there is a seedy part in which a certain kind of clientele seems to find their niche; New Rio was no different. Usually you would look for housing that has seen better days, with small businesses that don't add up too much and are prevalent only in that part of town. It usually starts with pawnshops and tattoo parlors. New Rio was small enough that it rated only one of each. But for their purposes it was as good as any place to start. Buck walked into the pawnshop with Rachael. While Buck had the pawnshop owner's attention, Rachael looked the place over trying to find something that would give away the clientele/customer's whereabouts. After getting nowhere with the pawnshop owner, Buck waited for Rachael outside and a little down the street. When she appeared, she kept walking past Buck to the truck. Once at the truck they got in. Buck was puzzled by Rachael's actions.

However, before he could say anything, Rachael started saying, "You were right to check the local dives; the stuff the pawnshop owner has is all hot."

Buck looked puzzled by her statement. "How do you know it's all hot?"

"The serial numbers on the big stuff have been scratched out and given new numbers. The new serial numbers looked as if they were done professionally and if you're not trained to look for it, you wouldn't know they were changed. Only on the big purchase items were the serial numbers new, but nonetheless all bad numbers."

With this new information Buck and Rachael went back into the pawnshop and asked again for the owner. The owner came from his office in the back, appearing a little nervous this time. Buck let Rachael run the interrogation by asking all of the questions. After identifying herself as FBI, she asked to see the paperwork for the high-value stuff in the store. After looking over the paperwork she threw it in the air much to the surprise of the owner. She then asked to see the real paperwork, not this made-up stuff. By now the pawnshop owner was starting to get really nervous.

Buck stepped in, "Do we need to get a warrant for this place?"

Rachael thought for a second. "Could be, depends on the owner here."

By now the pawnshop owner was starting to mumble to himself; you could see the fear in his eyes.

Rachael looked at him, "Where did this stuff come from?"

The owner wasn't quite ready to talk just yet.

"How many years in prison can you get for handling stolen property?" Buck asked.

"Depends on how long and how much and where it came from," Rachael said.

"So, you're saying five maybe ten years."

This time Rachael slammed her fist down on the counter and yelled, "Where did you get this stolen stuff?"

By now the resolve of the pawnshop owner was gone. At first he claimed he had no idea the stuff was stolen. To which Buck looked at Rachael saying, "Maybe he didn't know."

Rachael thought about this for a minute. "Could be; either way, someone has to go to jail though. You know the judge won't care."

By now the owner was ready to talk. Buck asked him about the stolen articles and how he got them.

"A guy shows up with the stuff and wants to get rid of it," the owner stated.

"You don't ask any questions when buying this stuff?" Rachael asked.

"I just buy the stuff, no questions asked," the owner said.

"Because you didn't ask you're now going to jail," Rachael replied.

"Who did you buy this stuff from? What did they look like?" Buck asked.

By now the owner was ready to change his clothes due to how scared he was and his cool demeanor was now gone. He started choking on his words and sweating.

This time Buck grabbed him by the front of his shirt and slammed him up against the counter yelling into his face, "No more chances; talk or you're getting locked up now."

Whatever resolve the pawnshop owner had was gone; he started talking almost in confusion. Rachael had to slow him down to understand what he was saying.

"These guys show up every once in a while with stuff they want to pawn. I look it over and give them money for it, no questions asked. Then I make up the serial numbers to make it legal." the owner claimed.

"Do you have any pictures of these guys?" asked Buck, still in his face.

"No, but I have security cameras for the day-to-day operation," the owner said.

At this time Rachael asked, "Can we see the footage from the cameras?"

Buck loosened his grip on the owner as he motioned to the back of the store, where there was a separate office. Buck now let go of his shirt and collar. The owner almost tripped as he took them to his back office.

"When was the last time they were here?" Rachael asked.

The owner said sometime last week, nervously. At this time Buck went to grab him again.

This time the owner cringed, waiting for Buck, and yelled, "Last Tuesday!"

Buck moved back to where he was before. Rachael looked at the dates on the DVDs and found Tuesday and popped it into the DVD player. As she ran through the DVD she saw people coming in with some merchandise to pawn and she slowed the DVD down to a normal speed.

By now all were watching the DVD display, Buck looked at it and said, "Well, what do you know."

"Bingo." Rachael agreed.

The figures on the DVD screen were the two guys, Hernandez and Martinez, the guys in the chase cars for Jim.

Buck and Rachael looked at the pawnshop owner with Buck asking, "How long have you been doing business with Hernandez and Martinez?"

"About six months now," the owner replied.

"What else were they bringing in here to sell?" asked Rachael.

The owner, quite a bit calmer now, replied, "Drugs."

"What kind of drugs?" asked Buck.

"Meth, heroin, speed and mushrooms."

With the DVD still playing Rachael caught something in the corner of the screen and stopped the DVD, reversed it a few frames, watching the screen intently. About a second into the play she called Buck over to watch the screen. They both see Jim standing in the back of one of the isles with his gun drawn. Hernandez and Martinez weren't aware of Jim being there. Jim watched what was going on and kept his gun drawn on the two. Then Martinez and Hernandez left the store. Jim walked up to the owner with his gun still drawn and asked the owner to cough up what the two had delivered. The owner laid out two plastic wrapped bundles of drugs and some cash. Jim grabbed the bundles and the money then exited the store and headed away from the front of the store.

At this point Buck pulled out his handcuffs and placed the owner under arrest and read him his rights. Rachael called Evans asking for a squad car to come to the pawnshop for a pick-up. Rachael started picking up the DVDs from the case and packed them into a plastic bag for evidence and processing. Evans showed up with his own vehicle and threw the owner into the back of the Suburban. Both Rachael and Buck talked to Evans, telling him what they found inside the pawnshop.

Evans looked relieved. "Finally, a break in the case."

Foster heard the call from Rachael on his police radio and came driving up in his car. Wondering what's going on, he asks Buck, "What's up?"

After a few minutes talking to Buck he too is excited to hear about the good news. After Buck processed the pawnshop owner for receiving stolen goods and dealing with the distribution of drugs with intent to sell, Buck closed the cell door behind him and walked away.

"Everything keeps coming back to Jim. Where is he hiding?" Rachael asked.

Buck looked at her and smiled as he said, "You're beautiful when you're thinking out loud."

Rachael pretended not to hear but smiled anyway. After a more formal briefing about the pawnshop owner being arrested and booked for his part in the selling of the drugs and receiving stolen goods, all attention turned to trying to figure out how Jim played a part in all of this.

"Where is Jim and how do we find him?" Foster asked.

"That is the 64 thousand dollar question," Evans replied.

They all agreed that the new focus would be on Jim and how to get him, assuming he was still alive. With one purpose in mind the team functioned as a well-oiled machine with one goal and that was to find Jim. Foster now seemed more determined to find Jim no matter what it took. He started by talking to his counterparts in the state gang section for more information about the mafia in Phoenix and who they did business with when it came to selling drugs. Evans and Rachael started calling in all of their IOUs from their counterparts inside and outside the FBI to locate Jim and the activities of the cartels in the state. Buck was getting ready to interrogate the pawnshop owner to see if he had any information about Jim that was relevant to their case but decided to hold off until he had a chance to review the security disc footage to see if anything else might turn up that would help in the interrogation. The pawnshop owner was going to have to wait until the review of the security discs was complete. The good thing about the pawnshop owner was he was locked up and awaiting federal charges. Buck thought to himself that with this kind of leverage against the owner he might be willing to turn states evidence against Jim to keep from going to jail.

With all the new activity going on, the team seemed happily engaged in their jobs, checking and rechecking their sources for anything that would point them in the right direction to find Jim.

Buck had been sitting for almost four hours reviewing the security discs trying to find anything about Jim and his whereabouts. Rachael came in after her review of her sources to assist Buck in reviewing the discs, mainly to keep him awake and from losing his focus. The security discs showed nothing new; however, they did see the vehicle that Jim drove to the pawnshop pass by every other day as if he was waiting for someone to show. The pawnshop owner was in about 90% of the footage. Only one other time did Martinez and Hernandez show up, each time carrying a duffle bag. The pawnshop owner would pay cash to the two guys each time they showed up.

At this time Foster came forward with the news that Jim was most likely still alive somewhere in the Phoenix area. The gang task unit found that some activity was taking place in and around the Glendale/Peoria area. The unit said it looked as if someone was recruiting for a take-over of the Mafia. No names as of yet but still active for the area. Foster knew that Glendale was considered to be open ground for the taking as was Peoria. The gang who had this area could control all of northern Phoenix and the surrounding areas. More of a white-collar bedroom community, which had enough money and businesses to support itself, it could be quite lucrative for the drug trade. The potential was there to make it worth a shot to go after the drug business. As was the custom, the existing gangs had first call on the new areas; however, it wasn't written in stone. Once again, whoever had the firepower and people could and would control the business. From the unit's view, it looked as if someone was cutting into the game and was willing to kill the competition and do whatever it took to make it theirs. So far, no bodies had turned up but it was just a matter of time before there would be a turf war over the new territory.

The unit had contacted the Phoenix police to let them know what was going on and to be on the lookout for new players in the area. The description of Jim had been forwarded to all of the local police departments with Foster waiting to follow up on any leads. The FBI had also been made aware of Jim and information was slowly being fed back to Evans and Rachael.

It seemed Jim had come from Chicago about 16 months ago to settle in New Rio. With no criminal record, he was able to get a job at the bank as a teller, which would provide good cover for all other activities he may have been involved in. It was as if Jim was conducting a fact-finding tour of the operations and layout before committing the organization from Chicago. Jim had been their point man into a new area of business in New Rio. The money laundering was just the beginning for the Chicago operations. Jim took an active part in the drug trade for the New Rio area. He was committing Chicago into the drug-trafficking operations and making inroads into the drug cartel in Arizona. This would require Chicago to come in with their people and take over the business from the mafia. Fortunately for Chicago, the desert could hide the bodies from ever being found. The interesting fact was this was a big step for Chicago to get a foothold in a multibillion-dollar business in Arizona and possibly all the way into California. Chicago was going to step on the toes of the mafia and the cartels in order to break into the drug business. This would require Chicago to depend on the members of the other syndicates to play along. The enticement would be the millions of dollars that lined the pockets of the cartel and the mafia. Controlling the gangs and dealers would cover every aspect of the drug trade. The Chicago syndicate was cutting into and trying to monopolize the whole US drug trade. The FBI and other federal agencies were watching with a keen interest as was the unit waiting to see what would happen next.

With this newfound knowledge everybody on the team knew what was at stake. Jim Olds had to be found and stopped or innocent people were likely to die as collateral damage in a war that could last for years. The body count could go on and on.

The strangle hold of the drug trade could be used to destroy anybody or any organization that stood up to the syndicate. The U.S. would have its own cartel operating within its borders with power and influence to stop any police and/or federal agency. The realignment of power would be absolute and very well-organized from within the confines of the U.S. The price of the drugs would be controlled by the whims of the syndicate. The middleman would not be needed by this setup of power within the Chicago organization. The organizations involved in this type of operation would be tantamount to a government with its own military enforcement. The battle would be of good versus evil with the outcome being controlled by whatever force was strong enough to enforce their rule.

At this time Buck and Rachael were on the verge of both falling asleep from watching the security discs. Nothing had come from the discs to reinforce anything they hadn't already known. By now it was late and time for something to eat to break the boredom of sitting for long hours of watching TV. Evans and Foster were ready to go as well. The sum total of their work wouldn't be seen for some time. The intelligence arena was not known for being fast but more for being thorough before acting on any information. Slow and effective was more important than fast and loose. They all knew that with big brother now watching it would take time for all of the pieces to fit together to create a plan to stop what had begun. How to stop the syndicate and the other resources from taking over the drug trade in America and possibly taking down the U.S. government without creating a panic or something worse was the paramount thought in the minds of the key players and their agencies. How to do it covertly without bursting the bubble of public complacency of being safe and secure in America was the key issue. Panic and fear was the problem that now faced the intelligence community. This had been learned from dealing with terrorist attacks in the United

State; it can happen but only in isolated cases.

The team all went to the local café for dinner and, as they ate their food, the quiet was loud enough to deafen the room supplied with the thoughts running through their minds. How do you find a needle in a field of haystacks when you're not sure which field to look in? The key was to find Jim Olds and stop the syndicate from starting a war across the U.S.

Buck started the conversation by telling the others that nothing of value showed up in the security discs, Rachael nodded in agreement. Foster and Evans gave a short brief as to what they had been doing in contacting the federal agencies and waiting for their inputs to assist in nailing Jim before it was too late. Foster stirred his coffee with his spoon in lazy circles as everybody was deep in thought. Each trying to run down their own checklist in their heads trying to make sure they hadn't missed anything.

Buck spoke first. "All I have left to do is interrogate the pawnshop owner, although I'm not expecting anything new from the interrogation."

"Nothing ventured, nothing gained," Evans stated.

With that they all agreed.

"Has anybody done a record check of all of the stuff from the pawnshop?" Foster asked.

"I'll handle that tomorrow morning. It shouldn't take too long to verify what was stolen," Rachael said.

"I'm tired and ready to head back to my room to get some sleep," Foster added.

"I'm headed that way myself. We've done all we can do at this point," Evans agreed.

Nobody said anything. It was now a case of waiting to see what would bear fruit.

Buck offered to take Rachael back to her place on his way home. Rachael thought that would be nice.

As they approached her place, Rachael asked Buck, "Do you want to come in for a minute or two?"

"Why not."

As Rachael opened her door she stood there for a moment surveying the room. Nothing was out of place but she couldn't help but feel as if something was not right. Buck followed her in and sensed her reluctance to be there.

Buck took her out of the room. "You're staying with me tonight."

With that, she gathered some of her belongings and headed back out the door with Buck. When they reached his place, Buck went in first to check it out. Finding nothing wrong, Rachael went in. Buck cleared the bed in his room for her to sleep on and made his way to the couch with his pillow and blanket.

"I feel like a scared little girl, feeling inadequate about being in her own apartment," Rachael stated.

"Not to worry; if you hear any low growling it was just me snoring."

Rachael laughed at this and got herself ready for bed by closing the door to his bedroom. Buck made himself comfortable on the old couch and was asleep in minutes.

The next morning was a typical day in New Rio; the sky was clear and blue with no clouds. The morning was cool and the desert was beautiful with cactus flowers starting to bloom. The colors of the flowers were always bold and stood out against the prickly pear cactus ears so pretty, but don't touch for fear of being stuck with the needles. The morning woke Buck up to the smell of eggs and toast being cooked, with some bacon sizzling in the fry pan. He came into the kitchen to see Rachael in her pajamas cooking, she turned to see Buck standing there and asked, "Are you ready for breakfast?"

Buck looked at her for a second. Smiling. "I could get used to this."

Rachael smiled in return walking over to him and kissing him. "You need to get cleaned up before I do; I may take a little longer."

With that, he headed into the bathroom to take a shower and shave.

Buck and Rachael were the last to arrive at the office and were ready to start the interrogation with the pawnshop owner. As they made their way to the holding cell, Foster and Evans were sitting in their chairs trying to wake up. Foster was on his second cup of coffee and Evans was still sipping on his first cup. Both of them looked up to see Rachael and Buck as they came in. Buck couldn't help but feel sorry and admiration for both of them. Being away from home and family had started to take a toll on them; you could see it in their faces. Yet they were doing their jobs without complaint. They both knew what was at stake. Their way of life and their families being safe and secure was paramount in their minds. Buck went to the holding cell to get the pawnshop owner while Rachael cleared the interrogation room to use. Buck brought the pawnshop owner to the room, where Rachael handcuffed him to the table. While this was happening Buck looked over his file notes for the pawnshop owner. He reviewed the arrest record that had been put together and noted that this wasn't the first time the owner had a run-in with the law, and shared this information with Rachael.

Rachael looked the owner over before starting the interrogation.

"According to our records here, you've been in trouble before with the law."

"Yes, but that was a long time ago."

Buck looked at him. "Assault with intent to do bodily harm is pretty serious stuff."

"I'd been minding my own business when this guy came up and started harassing me for my money. I said no to him several times before I hit him."

"Yes, that's what the report says here; it was the lead pipe you hit him with twice that got you in trouble," Buck said.

The owner got quiet after that.

"How much time did you get for that?" Rachael asked.

"A year in county lockup in Maricopa County."

"Sheriff Mike says hi to ya," Buck said.

The owner smirked at him, thinking to himself what he would like to do to Buck.

Buck looked at the pawnshop owner. "Your next stint in jail will be for a lot longer time and in real prison."

"You might see some of your customers in there, you never know," Rachael added.

The pawnshop owner knew this to be true and, without thinking twice, asked what he could do to help himself out.

Buck looked at Rachael. "What can you give us about Jim Olds?"

"All I know about this guy Jim is, he shows up wanting to cut in on the action of the Mafia and said if I didn't play he would kill me."

"How did he know about what you were doing?" Rachael asked.

"I don't know how he knew, you got to believe me."

"How did he know when the guys would come to you?" Rachael asked.

"It was prearranged when they were coming."

"That still doesn't answer my question."

The owner was starting to get upset. "He must have been watching me for a while."

"What would they bring to you and what would you give them?" asked Buck.

"I was a drop-off point for the money and drugs."

"Where did you get the money?"

"The money came from up north, from previous drug sales. The people from up north would come down to get the drugs and head back."

Buck stood up and leaned into the owner's face. "You're telling me that all you were was a go between north and south Arizona for drugs and money?"

"My take was that I'd make enough to keep me quiet and enjoy living in New Rio, especially with the local cops oblivious to what was going on in their own backyard. The Mafia knew that as long as they kept it cool, no one would be the wiser for it."

"Just about worked, didn't it?" said Rachael.

"All I know is Jim showed up and basically took over the whole setup, and I started working for him without telling the Mexicans about it."

Buck was embarrassed by his reply, but didn't say anything. Buck had been had by the local town trash. The owner knew he was going away for a long time and wouldn't be coming back.

"Until it was too late for them," Rachael interjected.

The owner nodded in agreement.

"How did it go down for your points of contact, Martinez and Hernandez?" Buck asked.

"It was set up by Jim; he had people following the two from the get go; they were waiting for the right time to take the money and drugs. Jim knew when they would be most vulnerable for the heist."

"What was in California and why was Jim headed there?" asked Buck.

"I think he thought if he could find out who was running the show in California, he could take them out as well by doing the same thing he did here in New Rio and jack their stuff as well."

"How many were with him on the way to California?" asked Rachael.

"I don't know, but he had at least three people with him at all times."

Rachael left the room and talked to Evans to find out if anything else showed up from the California shootings.

"Nothing as of yet," Evans replied.

Buck waited for Rachael to come back into the room before going on any further.

"This Jim is a pretty smart bastard and greedy too. I think Jim is pushing for control by starting a war with the other gangs taking the hit for his work," Buck said.

Rachael nodded in agreement with him.

Both Buck and Rachael looked at each other and agreed the owner couldn't help them anymore at this point. With that, Jim Olds was still out there two steps in front of them and getting farther away.

As they led the pawnshop owner back to the holding cell, Buck looked at Rachael and tilted his head a little to signal her that he had an idea. Rachael caught his eyes and waited to see what would happen next.

As Buck put the owner in the cell, he said out loud, "Looks like you're going down for the murders of Hernandez and

Martinez. With Jim still out there you're going down by yourself."

By now Rachael understood what was happening and added, "Double homicide, premeditated murder. That could be the death sentence or at least life with no parole."

The look of shock on the owner's face was priceless and what you would call a Kodak moment. The owner started raising his voice as Buck and Rachael walked away.

This time the owner yelled out, "Wait, you can't pin those murders on me!"

Rachael stopped and turned around, speaking softly. "Why not, you knew what was going down and you did nothing to stop it. That makes you an accomplice in the murders."

Buck looked at the owner. "You're wasting your breath; you're going down as if you pulled the trigger yourself."

By now the owner was getting pretty upset about all of this. At this point he looked at Rachael and pleaded, "I want to make a deal."

"You don't have anything to make a deal with," Buck replied.

"I know more than you think."

This time Rachael said, "Like what."

"I have an idea where Jim is holing up and where he is going."

"The clock is ticking," Buck said.

The owner looked as if he were going to have a heart attack.

"Jim is waiting to bring in more of his people from Chicago and other members from the other organizations to start their takeover!" he yelled.

"Tell us something we don't know," Buck said.

"I was working with Jim from the get go. I worked with him because I got tired of dealing with the Mexicans. They were always trying to cheat me, and I knew they were going to kill me if and when they had a chance."

"Boohoo," said Rachael.

"You don't understand. Jim came to me with his plan and asked if I was willing to help in the takeover of the drug business.

Jim and I staged what you saw on the security discs. Jim and I have been setting up this operation now for over a year. Basically, he was trying to get control of the drugs and money for the takeover. We had been watching what the Mafia had been doing in order to know where and when to strike."

"What about the bank robbery?" asked Buck.

"That was done by someone else that was above and beyond our control."

"That doesn't make sense," said Rachael. "Jim worked at the bank; his wife is one of the victims."

Buck looked surprised by all of this. "Why were Whitey and Ritchins sent down here from the same organization that sent Jim?"

Now the owner was in deeper trouble just for admitting he was being part of the plan. He didn't pull the trigger; however, he knew what was going to happen. The only consolation was that two bad guys were taken out by other bad guys.

Buck and Rachael went back to their desks and tried to take in everything that the pawnshop owner had told them.

Buck looked at Rachael. "Well, what do we do now?"

Rachael paused for a moment deep in thought. "We got everything else we needed but not the reason for the bank robbery."

"We got the reasons for Hernandez and Martinez being killed but not the wife of Jim or the old man with the truck," Buck said.

When Evans and Foster walked in and sat down at the table, Buck and Rachael told them what they had learned from the pawnshop owner.

"Do you think Jim is acting on his own?" Evans asked.

Foster answered his question, "I believe he is acting in behalf of Chicago; elsewise, why would they support him in killing the two Mafia guys?"

By now one case was almost solved but not the original case that brought them together.

"Where do we look now?" Buck asked.

"I believe Jim is still in the area; he got what he wanted. He's got a toehold into the drug business in New Rio and some support from the local people; i.e., the pawnshop owner, and his own enforcers to make it happen. I don't believe he is going to walk away from all of this. I believe he wants to settle the score with whoever put out the hit for the robbery and the murder of his wife," Rachael said.

"Somebody knew about the money being laundered besides Chicago and I think he is looking for that somebody now. I believe he is looking for that connection with the Mafia or the cartel, and with the backing of Chicago, what's to stop him? The question still stands, where is Jim and what is his next move going to be?" Buck chimed in.

"If you wanted to take control of a drug operation and weren't concerned about the fallout, what would you do to infiltrate and disrupt the business?" Foster asked.

"I would do what Jim has done by starting with New Rio and moving my people into key positions of the local power grid. I would get rid of people by taking over their operations, by killing the pushers and suppliers at the local level without disrupting the flow of drugs coming in. I feel that is what he's doing right now," Rachael answered.

Foster looked at everybody and said, "Maybe it's time to check into the Mafia drug network."

With that, he was back on the phone talking to the gang task force, asking about the network of the Monterrey Mafia here in Arizona.

"Which cartel supplies the drugs to the Mafia?" Buck asked Evans.

"The Monterrey Cartel, they are based primarily in Monterrey, Mexico.

"What do you know about them?"

"The Monterrey Cartel is known for their drug trafficking, money laundering, and organized crime syndicate. It is associated with the label "Golden Triangle," which refers to the states of Sinaloa, Durango, and Chihuahua. The area is a major producer of Mexican opium and marijuana. The Cartel is responsible for importing into the United States and distributing nearly 200 tons of cocaine and large amounts of heroin. They have been actively involved in smuggling illicit drugs into the United States and trafficking them throughout the country."

When Evans finished, Buck stood there amazed at what he had heard. After taking a minute to digest what Evans, said he asked, "Where do we go from here?"

"Jim is playing with fire when it comes to the Monterrey Cartel. I think it has to do with what networks the Chicago organization comes up with to distribute the products that will make this cartel want to deal with them and Jim. The bottom line is the money that is generated by whoever sells the most products. This will determine who survives and who doesn't as far as trafficking goes," Evans said.

The Mafia based here in Arizona is a group who patterned themselves after the California Mafia which is based in the prison system and has been in existence for several years. Several Hispanics who came into the Arizona prison system brought the concept and philosophy of the California Mafia with them. The rules are as follows:

1. A member can't be an informant, or rat.

2. A member can't be a coward.

3. A member can't raise a hand against another member without approval.

4. A member can't show disrespect for any member's family, including sex with another member's wife, or girlfriend.

5. A member can't steal from another member.

6. A member can't be homosexual.

7. A member can't politic against another member or cause dissension within the organization.

8. Membership is for life.

9. It's mandatory to assault or kill all dropouts.

10. The eMe (gang) comes first. Even before your own family.

11. A member can't interfere with another member's business activities.

The Mafia is the controlling organization for almost every Hispanic gang in Southern California. Members of a lot of Hispanic gangs in Southern California are obliged under the threat of death to carry out any and all orders."

"That explains why Jim was headed to California when we followed him," Buck exclaimed.

"Now you know why everybody is interested in what Jim is doing. If he pulls this off, a civil war will come to fruition and people on both sides will die. If it was just the bad guys, dying you wouldn't hear too much crying from the law-enforcement community. That being said, it never is clean and somebody that isn't even involved with drugs or gangs is going to get hurt," Foster added.

"What makes Jim think he can get away with this?" asked Buck.

"Don't know; all I know is the ramifications are pretty serious, to say the least," Foster said.

By now Rachael and Evans were listening to what Foster was saying and they all agreed that Jim had to be stopped from carrying out his plans.

# CHAPTER X

As Buck stood there thinking about this entire scenario, he started to think, if I was Jim where would I go to get off the radar, especially near New Rio. Buck looked at the map that was still hanging on the whiteboard. He used his finger to trace some of the mountain topography nearby, hoping to find something that would indicate where Jim could be. He knew of the old mines in the area; they could in some cases be used as places to hole up in. With water and food, you could stay hidden or gone for quite a while, and no one would be the wiser for it. Some of the mines were big enough you could park an ATV inside.

While Buck was looking at the map Evans received an e-mail about the key that was found in Jim's apartment. Evans let Buck read the e-mail, and as he read it, he could tell it wasn't good news. The e-mail read as follows: Based upon the information from the FBI lab, the key could fit just about anything that had a lock attached to it, most likely it would fit a heavy-duty strong box.

With this new information the question now was, where would you hide a strong-box? Maybe in a cave or maybe a mine shaft in the desert or maybe under a floorboard in a house, who knows where? By this time Buck was feeling frustrated.

Rachael could see it in his eyes and quickly walked over to him, "Let's go for a ride."

Buck sensing he was about to explode, gratefully said, "I could use it right now."

As they walked out of the office, Buck told Rachael, "We have old mines in the desert big enough to live in, if needed, and if properly stocked, you could stay out there in the desert for quite some time."

"Where are they located?"

Buck raised his hands pointing to the desert. "Out there."

Rachael took this to mean that the desert was covered with old mines pretty much everywhere.

Buck gestured to the south end of town. "Most of the old mines are south of New Rio about 10 maybe 12 miles from here."

"Are you sure this is feasible? Better yet, are there any other gangs or gang members here in the area that would want a piece of the action if the Mafia were out of the picture?"

Buck hadn't thought of this before. "I don't know of anyone else here in the area right offhand."

Rachael had gotten Buck to thinking about another option. With that in mind Buck said, "I know of one old mine out here that is worth checking, just to satisfy my curiosity."

"What are we waiting for?"

With that, they told Evans and Foster about their intentions to find this old mine.

Rachael asked Foster to look into any other gangs/members in the area that might stand to gain if the Mafia was out of the drug business.

"Will do, shouldn't take too long," Foster said.

With that taken care of Rachael told Evans they shouldn't be gone too long out in the desert; however, if they weren't back in a couple of hours to come looking for them.

"Always the fun jobs for you two," Evans smiled.

Rachael and Buck smiled and both nodded and headed out the door.

Buck had known the area were the mines were since he was a kid in grade school. He and his friends would go out once in a while to explore the mines and shafts for fun. They knew the mines could be dangerous but that was the adventure of it all. What if they found gold or some old prospector's stuff in one of the old mines? That was the thrill of the hunt for the boys. One time they found an old coal shovel and some lanterns left behind by the miners. The hard-rock mines were the safest to explore, there was no chance of a cave in. The only thing you needed to have was hard hats in case you busted your head on the low overhang. With flashlights and ropes no mine was exempt from being explored. Every weekend if not playing sports or with the girls, the guys and Buck would head out to find their next treasure trove. In all actuality, nothing of value was ever found in the old mines; it was the thrill of the hunt that made it worthwhile. Only once did they run into problems. One shaft they were exploring was filled with methane gas, and when they lit some candles they heard a small rumble down deep in the mine. That had been their cue to get out of the mine fast; fortunately, no one was hurt. When the smoke cleared from the entrance of the mine, the boys sat down and made a count of all their stuff. With the exception of a few flashlights and some courage, they were all in one piece. One mine they found was filled with water and some old wooden barrels, the kind they used for whiskey. They were mostly empty, but the temptation to drink some of the remaining alcohol was too much. It took a couple of hours for them to get back lugging one of the barrels of whiskey home. None of them could remember anything after they had a drink of it (evidently it was pretty good stuff). Now, 15 years later, it was Buck and Rachael searching the desert for the mines. Rachael sat enthralled by the stories that Buck told of his youth and exploring the old mines.

"Watch out for animals or spiders inside the old mines. The tarantulas can jump quite a ways straight up, in fact, in your face. Ask me how I know this," Buck told Rachael.

Rachael smiled and drew closer to Buck for protection. At this Buck smiled, "Do the itty-bitty spiders scare the big tough FBI agent?"

Rachael turned and playfully hit him. "Not as long as I have my gun, flame thrower and a couple of flashbangs with me."

They both chuckled at her comment.

When they arrived at the mine, Buck parked his truck about a quarter mile away, trying not to let anybody who might be around know they were there. They walked the last bit of the way in the dark without turning on their flashlights, just to be sure not to alert anybody out in the desert who might be close by. It took some time to make their way to the mine that Buck wanted to check out. The moon didn't help at all this night, hiding behind the clouds and peeking out once in a while, had hindered their progress. Once there, the mine shaft was quite large. Rachael was surprised by its size. Buck turned on his flashlight to look inside and walked in through the opening. A couple of bats flew out of the entrance of the cave.

Buck looked back at Rachael. "Oh, I forgot about the bats."

Rachael looked at him with a questioning look. "I bet you did."

"Don't you worry; they won't suck your blood."

At this point Rachael turned on her flashlight as well and moved closer to Buck. They were inside the mine shaft about 25 feet when they saw the bodies of three people.

"Stay put for a minute, until I call you," Buck told Rachael.

Rachael looked at him. "The hell I am."

"Well, come on then."

It looked as if the bodies had only been there a short time. Buck didn't recognize any of them. He could tell they were Latinos but not from around New Rio.

"It looks as if they were shot from behind," Rachael said.

Buck agreed with her observations. Rachael took out her phone and took their pictures and sent them to Evans and Foster to identify. The bodies each had tattoos on their arms and hands, which Rachael took pictures of as well.

"Maybe the tats will identify who they are and where they came from," Rachael said.

Buck continued to walk deeper into the mine while Rachael was taking pictures. A little deeper into the mine Buck called out to Rachael, asking her to come into the mine where he was. As she walked further into the mine to meet Buck, she noticed that the mine was getting cooler the farther she walked in. When she found Buck, she was glad he was there to keep her warm. Buck told Rachael to shine her light into the deeper part of the darkness. After doing so, she gasped in surprise as the light finally fell onto the interior walls of the cave. She stood there trying to identify what she was looking at. There was a lifeless body hanging from the rock. It looked as if the individual had been tortured to death. The face was completely gone and his body had been tied with his legs and hands stretched out across the cave.

"Who is he?" Rachael asked.

"I don't know; I thought it may have been Jim, but it's not. You can tell by the tattoos on his arms."

Rachael took more pictures of the body and sent them to Foster and Evans once again.

Foster called Rachael on her phone. "What is going on out there; did you guys find a cemetery?"

"I think so; you better send out the forensics team on this one."

Buck kept looking around the cave using his flashlight. Rachael started doing the same with hers.

"How deep is this mine?" Rachael asked.

"It's been so long since I was here I don't remember."

With that, they continued deeper into the cave. They did find empty containers of food and empty gallon water jugs littered all around the place.

"What I think we found is a staging area for illegals coming into the state, possibly mules for the drug trade. I suspect the one that was tortured was the leader of the group and the other three were the enforcers. From my understanding the drug business is pretty risky for the mules. I'm thinking the load they were carrying was stolen from the original mules and taken by another group," Buck said.

"Jim?"

"Could be; at this point I wouldn't put it past him. It could be some competition from another drug cartel. We'll know more after forensics and the medical examiner gets done with their checks."

As Buck and Rachael left the cave, Rachael contacted Foster and Evans with directions to the cave. As they walked back to the truck, the sun was starting to make its appearance over the mountains in the east. They sat and waited for Foster and Evans to show up with the medical examiner and the forensics team. Buck sat in the truck, realizing for the first time how brutal the drug business was and is. Jim was no better than his opponents in this game of money and power. People were the pawns and could be easily replaced by others who were desperate to have the money or the promise of a new life in a better place with nothing to lose and everything to gain.

Buck spoke out loud, "What are you willing to do for the almighty American dollar?"

Rachael was lost in her own thoughts as well, thinking to herself about the waste of life in the cave. Four people were dead trying to get ahead in life, and for all their work they were in the cave dead.

"What was it all for?" she said to herself.

Both Buck and Rachael didn't say anything until Foster and Evans showed up.

At this point both were tired of being up all night and ready to go back to bed to recover from it all. The visions they had of the dead bodies were seen every time they closed their eyes. Both had seen death before but not like this. People had been murdered and tortured for what? The dead were the only ones who knew why and how come. When Foster walked out of the cave, he went to one of the sides and threw up. Evans was just as silent when he returned to where Buck and Rachael were. Foster regained his composure and walked back to the group as well.

"And you wonder why we do what we do. Senseless, totally senseless," Foster said.

"We've got to stop this; even if it's just here, we need to stop this from ever happening again," Evans said.

The ride back to the office was quiet for Buck and Rachael. More tired than upset, there was nothing to say. Rachael moved closer to Buck and laid her head on his shoulder and pretended to sleep. Buck was glad she was there, even asleep. Last night would take some time to get over for both of them.

When they arrived back in New Rio, Buck walked Rachael to her apartment and was about to leave when Rachael asked if he would stay a while with her. He thought, he didn't want to be alone either, and said he would. They both lay on the bed fully exhausted and just held each other till they both went to sleep. For the moment they had each other and they would get through this eventually, and that was all they needed for now.

# CHAPTER XI

It was 6:00 pm when Buck started stirring from his sleep, as he opened his eyes he could see that Rachael was still asleep. Not wanting to wake her, he gently moved off of the bed and walked into the little kitchen and called Foster.

"I'm checking in to let you know we're still alive and to see if anything new has been found."

"Nothing new as far as the bodies went. We think they were mules, like you said, but to be certain we need to contact the Mexican police to be able to identify them, tats and all."

"Did they find anything inside the cave besides the bodies that would be worthwhile in our case against Jim?"

"It looks like a separate incident from what we've been working on. I think you need to stay out of the desert, leastwise till we solve the case with Jim," Foster jokingly said.

"It looks as if you've got job security for quite a while just in the county," Foster chuckled. "The fun keeps coming your way."

Buck agreed with that. "Too much fun for me. Let me speak to Evans for a minute."

Evans came to the phone. "Hello, how's Rachael doing?"

"She's still asleep; do you need her?"

"No, just checking on her. We'll see you guys tomorrow in the a.m."

"Will do and thanks."

The next morning everybody was there, and Evans brought the paperwork from the medical examiner for the autopsies.

Evans spoke first. "The first impression was correct about the bodies found in the cave. They were mules making their way to Tucson via the desert. The cave was a drop-off point for the drugs and illegals coming across the border through the desert."

"What about the tattoos they had on their bodies?" Rachael asked.

"The tats showed they belonged to a rival cartel called Scarlet Snakes. This would explain why the bodies were found in such a gruesome way. I think the Monterrey Cartel was sending a message to any outsiders thinking about trying to take over their business," Foster answered.

"Does this help us in any way?" Buck asked.

"No, it doesn't. But it does say that Jim is in for a real hard time trying to take over any drug trade," said Evans.

"The Monterrey Cartel is pretty well up to speed as to what is going on this area," Foster said.

"Jim would have to have some real strong firepower to take over this part of Arizona and get away with it. The question is who and what are they counting on to help them in this?" Evans added, "Jim is, as you know, not doing this on his own. He has backing from someone or some group wanting to take over. I think this is bigger than the Chicago organization or any other organized crime syndicate we know of."

"Could it be that another cartel is involved with this?" Rachael asked.

"Looks that way with the dead bodies found in the cave. How extensive the operation is, is our biggest worry right now," Evans replied.

"Right," said Foster as he continued, "Until we know who we're dealing with, we are at their mercy on this."

"What about DEA or Alcohol, Tabaco and Firearms (ATF) helping us on this one?" Buck asked.

"DEA is interested in this as much as we are. Their sources say that the Scarlet Snakes Cartel is flexing their muscles to try and take some of the business away from the Monterrey Cartel. This could spread all of the way into the U.S. as far as drug delivery and distribution, with borders being wide open and people coming across by the droves. The Scarlet Snakes Cartel could be replacing the Monterrey Cartel dealers with their own people. If that's the case, the dealers are going to be at war for a while, a war which nobody wins. The supply and demand for the drugs here in the states is up into the billions of dollars each year. Everybody wants a piece of the action to retire early and live to talk about it. As long as there is a demand, the Mexicans and South Americans will supply the need," Foster continued.

"And the weapons to fight the war will be supplied by North Korea, Russia, China, Cuba, and even the U.S. As they say, worldwide arms dealing is good business for those who are willing to pay for it," Evans added.

"It looks as if we have opened a can of worms with the possibility of never being able to close it," Buck said.

"The FBI feels the same way about it; hence, they are sending another agent along with the DEA sending their Intel people to assist us with this new war. They should be showing up sometime today or tomorrow," Evans added.

"At this point we are to stand by until further notice," said Foster.

"With that, everybody has the day off," said Evans.

They all sat there not knowing what to do. They had been working the case for so long, and it had taken all of their time to get this far. They kind of felt guilty with nothing to do but wait for the others to show.

Buck decided to take Rachael on a picnic into the desert.

As they were making their way to the picnic spot, Rachael kept asking, "Are we there yet?"

"Just a little bit further."

This was really starting to get to Rachael. After another 30 minutes of walking she started asking the question again.

This time Buck stopped and looked at her and said with a smile, "Don't make me turn this trail around."

To which she smiled a sheepish grin. "Okay."

As they made their way down into a canyon, Rachael asked, "Is that a waterfall I hear?"

"Why, yes it is."

Now that her curiosity was piqued, she started looking around the trail. Just up ahead was a river that was moving slowly away from them. When they reached the bottom of the canyon, both Rachael and Buck looked up at the waterfall, which was about 50 feet up. Rachael just stood there, amazed at the size of the waterfall and how loud it was. The river was about 10 feet across and moving very slow. Up the river were places where the green grass met the river bank, just right for a picnic. Buck laid out the blanket and the food. Rachael just stood there fascinated that the desert could have something so beautiful and so majestic not visible to the eye from the top. Buck sat down and motioned for Rachael to join him on the blanket.

As she sat down, she kept looking at the river and waterfall. "How did you know about this place?"

"The story goes that in the days of the wild west some Comanche braves were chasing a trapper across the desert and he stumbled upon the trail we took down to the waterfall and river. The Indians couldn't find him because he hid behind the waterfall and waited for them to leave. The trapper stayed down here for quite some time and actually built a cabin not too far away from here. He never told anybody about what he'd discovered. This place is the best kept secret I know of."

"So how did you find it?"

"My buddies and I would take off into the desert hiking and go in different directions. One time we would go north out of town, next time we would head south, and so on. We found the trail and followed it down to here. We even found the old trapper's cabin. This is the place I would go to get away from it all, plenty of fresh water to drink and fish to catch from the stream to keep you from starving."

Rachael kept looking around and finally started eating her lunch, still in disbelief that anything could be this beautiful and serene. After a bit she lay out on the blanket and started to doze. The sun was warm and the sound of the river and waterfall was like a lullaby putting you to sleep. Buck did likewise and they enjoyed the afternoon together. About 6:00 pm Buck and

Rachael made their way back up the canyon to the truck and on to home.

Foster took the time to call his wife and kids to see how they were doing and let them know that he was all right and would be home shortly. Evans wasn't married, so he kind of hung around the motel watching some TV and went swimming in the motel pool. He had invited Foster to come over to swim, watch some football and drink beer. All in all, it was a good down time for everybody working the case.

The next day when the whole team assembled they were met by the new FBI agent and DEA Intel personnel. Evans introduced the FBI agent as Gang Intel Specialist, Linda Scharp, who had been working gangs for about five years. The DEA Intel people were introduced as Jeff Call and Wendy Chu. Their specialty was the cartels operating in the U.S. and their connections with the outlaw motorcycle gangs and street gangs who were the distributors to the pushers who in turn sold to the public. They were, as Evans would say, "Very well learned in their trade."

Linda Scharp started the briefing. "As you may have already guessed, the gangs are quite notorious all through the big cities. Now, because of the competition between the gangs, they are spreading out into the smaller towns and trying to control it from the border all the way to Canada. The drug pushers are trying to monopolize the drug trade by whatever means necessary, i.e. murder and turf wars to get more of the profit back into the hands of the distributor/cartel. They do this by controlling the distribution and the selling of drugs from the moment they are delivered from the cartel to the street. The actual distribution of the drug is handled by the outlaw motorcycle groups and Mafia and others who move it from the border to the bigger cities. The major interstate highways are their preferred way of delivery. For example, the drugs are moved up Interstate 15 with two cars tagging, one in front and the other behind, to

run interference in case the state troopers and local police are
anywhere near."

At the completion of Ms. Scharp's briefing she asked, "Are there any questions?"

"How do you control the flow?" Buck asked.

"We have people on the inside known as Confidential Informants (CIs) and others who are willing to make deals in order to stay out of prison. Every once in a while we get lucky by having the police and Immigration and Customs Enforcement (ICE) stop the drug distributors. When they realize they are in deep crap, they start talking and pass information on to us, mainly for more lenient sentencing. As you can see, there is no honor or loyalty in the drug business."

As there were no more questions, Linda Scharp closed out her brief, "There is a war going on in the U.S., and it is a war we can't afford to lose and by fighting this war we are making a difference, albeit a small one. If I didn't believe in it, I wouldn't be here now." With that she sat down.

Wendy Chu and Jeff Call proceeded from this point with their own brief. Wendy spoke first. As she was speaking, Jeff handed out photos of some of the work that the cartels did to enforce their rules. The pictures made their way amongst the group, and as each of them looked at the pictures you could see the look of surprise on their faces. The photos showed people who had been killed by the cartel henchmen. Some of them were hanging from an overpass with their heads lying on the ground below them. One picture showed the blue barrels filled with acid to burn and get rid of the bodies. One picture showed a Mexican policeman standing next to a body of another policeman he had just shot because he wasn't on the payroll of the cartel. One of the other pictures showed heads that had been chopped off sitting on the hood of a car with the trunk open showing the bodies stuck inside. When the pictures had made their way through the group, Wendy gathered them up and had Jeff post them to the whiteboard.

Wendy at this point started with the Monterrey Cartel. "The pictures you just reviewed were all the work of the cartel we are about to talk about. As you know, the cartels are pretty powerful and very much in control, not only in the areas where they operate but also the governments that supposedly run the country they operate in. What the cartels cannot buy they destroy or intimidate by threatening to kill other family members. When you look at the poverty of the regions in Mexico you realize that the money the cartels payout is better than starving to death or going without. The people are trying to live the American dream in their own towns and cities.

The cartels deliver their drugs via personal aircraft, submersible boats, big cargo ships, mules from Mexico, through airports, dead bodies you name it; the cartels have probably tried it. The war between the cartels is sporadic and intense at times.

The weapons they use range from Rocket Propelled Grenades (RPGs), Light Anti-Tank Weapons (LAWs), grenades, semi-automatic and automatic weapons, night-vision goggles, boats and submarines all supplied or built by the USA, North Korea, China, and some South American countries, Russia and their subordinate nations. All in all, they are very well armed for their defensive and offensive war.

Money laundering and the businesses they use to launder the money are all over Mexico and America, reaching all the way into Europe. Most of the companies being used for money laundering are legitimate businesses that could employ your family members and friends, all the while laundering millions of dollars for the cartels. Banks are used to transform drug money into clean money by loans both business and personal and large loans to start businesses or maintain the business. Every dollar used in the United States, unless it's directly from the mint, will have a residue of a drug on it. That's how pervasive the drug business has gotten. The cartels never have a problem finding willing people to assist them in transferring the drugs from Mexico to the USA; it is just a matter of living in squalor or trying for the American dream. You don't see people trying to get into Mexico to live the good life. In fact, some of the South American countries have guards standing on the cliffs next to the sea to kill anybody trying get into their country. The difference of working for yourself and working in the cartel is about 20,000 dollars a year for the security versus the average wage of 10,000 dollars per year with the Monterrey Cartel making three billion a year.

Diego Juarez is 50, which in narco-years is about 150. He is a quasi-mythical figure in Mexico. He has outlived enemies and accomplices alike, defying the implicit bargain of a life in the drug trade, in which the careers are glittering but brief and always terminate in prison or the grave. When Juan Estevan was Juarez's age, he had been dead for more than a decade. In fact, according to the Drug Enforcement

Administration, Juarez sells more drugs today than Estevan did at the height of his career. To some extent, this success is easily explained as America's "insatiable demand for illegal drugs" and is what drives the industry. It's no accident that the world's biggest supplier of narcotics and the world's biggest consumer of narcotics just happen to be neighbors. The Monterrey Cartel can buy a kilo of cocaine in the highlands of Colombia or Peru for around $2,000, and then watch it accrue value as it makes its way to market. In Mexico, that kilo fetches more than $10,000. Go across the border to the United States, and it could sell wholesale for $30,000. Break it down into grams to distribute retail, and that same kilo sells for upward of $100,000 — more than its weight in gold. And that's just cocaine. Among the Mexican cartels, the Monterrey Cartel is diversified and vertically integrated, producing and exporting marijuana, heroin and methamphetamine as well.

By most estimates, though, the Monterrey Cartel has achieved a market share of at least 40 percent and perhaps as much as 60 percent, which means that Diego Juarez's organization would appear to enjoy annual revenues of some $3 billion."

When Wendy was done, she looked around the room and stared into the eyes of the team. All of them couldn't believe what Wendy had told them the money and the murders and, of course, the role the U.S. played in all of this.

After a couple of minutes the shock of this new information wore off and Buck asked, "Are we winning in the drug wars?"

Jeff Call answered the question. "If we don't fight, we lose. Just think what it would be like if we didn't fight it. The prisons are full of people who sell and buy drugs, along with white collar criminals and assorted murderers, rapists, robbers, and pedophiles. Why don't you ask them who's winning. The problem with the cartel is that if it wasn't drugs like heroin, meth, marijuana, and other assorted vices like gambling and prostitution that they offer, it would be something else the people demand. These problems have been around for quite a long time, it isn't new; in fact, it's rather old. Ludlum was made with cocaine, if the disease didn't kill you, it would cure whatever you were taking it for and you wouldn't care. J. Edger Hoover allowed the syndicates to grow without interference from the FBI because he liked to gamble."

At this point Wendy interjected, "Besides, doesn't it feel good when you catch them at their own game? For us, if we intercept the money before they get their hands on it, we win because they gave it away for free. The best part is that the money we find goes to other police departments for new equipment and other things for good use. The draw of easy money for both sides is what we are concerned about more than the drugs themselves. We can't control the supposedly good guys getting dirty because of the amount of money involved; just look at Mexico and South America when it comes to corruption. When it gets into our judicial system, like it did in Chicago, and most of the judges were on the take, it can scare you. Look at all of the murders that occur in Chicago, most of which deal with the gangs fighting for turf and drugs."

Rachael added her thoughts about Chicago. "Chicago is where you vote early and often."

Everybody chuckled over what she said, but all knew it to be true. With that, everybody got up to stretch their legs and move about and get some more coffee.

Buck walked over to Jeff Call. "What do you know about this area of Arizona?"

Jeff called Wendy over and had Buck repeat the question. Both Jeff and Wendy thought about the question for a minute before offering their opinion.

Jeff spoke first by saying to Wendy, "Correct me if I'm wrong on this." Wendy shook her head yes and waited for Jeff to go on. "Well, the truth of it is we really don't have much more information than you do already for this area. We know the mafia is running everything in this area pretty tight. Evans briefed us about Jim and what he's trying to do here, I don't see it working without a lot of backup to assist in the takeover. Could it be done? Maybe, just maybe. How long will it last? No one knows for sure in this business. We thought the Monterrey Cartel would be wiped out by now from other organizations trying to take over. It just goes to prove that anything is possible in the drug business as long as you don't use your own product."

Wendy added, "This Jim is quite the character in play here. He has the guts to do it; I just wonder if he has all the backing he needs to see it through? Not only does he have to deal with the cartel, he has to deal with the Mafia and the dealers he's trying to eliminate in order to gain control of the trade. For sure he is not acting alone; someone else is calling all of the shots. My question is, is it here in the good ole USA, or is some other group from Mexico trying to take over the Monterrey Cartel?"

Buck thanked them for their input on Jim and walked over to Rachael. "Well, what you think about the briefing?"

"A lot of what they talked about I already knew, but the pictures brought it home as to the kind of people we're dealing with."

"They are a nasty bunch, aren't they?"

Foster came over with Evans. "Well, where do we go from here?"

Buck relayed what Jeff and Wendy said about Jim working with another cartel trying to take over.

Evans thought about this, "It makes perfect sense that another cartel is in the running for the takeover. That would explain a lot, and if that's the case, we've been looking at this the wrong way."

"Instead of looking at the syndicates here on this side of the border, we should look at who has the more to gain. There must be an invisible player we have not been aware of lurking in the background, calling all of the shots, with Jim doing the dirty work and waiting for the right time to take over," Foster suggested.

"We need to figure out who has the most to gain in this takeover. By doing so we may find out who Jim is working for. I feel that ultimately Jim is our key to solving all of this," Rachael said.

Foster and the others agreed with Rachael.

Buck now added in his two cents worth. "Where do we look for Jim and where do we start?"

"Where did we see him the last time?" Foster asked.

"He was on his way to California with the shipment of drugs and money," Buck answered.

Rachael thought out loud, "Maybe he's still in California then. Maybe he never left California."

"It could be he's still in California waiting for the heat to cool down before his next move," Foster stated.

With this thought Evans said, "If we figure out his next move, we could be there and nail his backside to the proverbial barn door."

Linda came over. "What barn door are you referring to?"

Evans and Foster brought Linda up to speed on their new thoughts of where Jim could be and what he may be doing after-wards.

"I meant to tell you about some gang killings down in Los Angeles over the past 48 hours. The people killed were part of the mafia and one of the distributors. They were shot execution style with two shots to the back of their heads." Linda said.

"Are there any clues as to who did it?" Evans asked.

"No, at this point all we know for sure is that the bodies were found stashed behind a dipsey dumpster."

"Who found them?" asked Rachael.

"Some kids were walking down the alley when they smelled the bodies, and I guess the bodies had been there all the time."

"Anything else you want to add?" Evans asked Linda.

She shook her head no. By now the team plus three started to think that Jim was pretty much hiding out in California. The bodies found could be the only clue they had for his whereabouts. With this, they started looking at anything that would give Jim away. It could be Jim isn't hiding out in California and is trying to orchestrate a takeover with the local gangs. He could do this by pitting the gangs against each other with promises of big payouts to the ones that win the battle. If Jim was able to organize the gangs for the takeover, he may be able to actually accomplish his designs of having a new cartel taking over the drug trade. The cartels would be in a fight for control of the drug business with no way to sell or distribute the drugs without the street gangs being there. With the street gangs changing their allegiance to another cartel the Monterrey Cartel would be out of business, drug rich and money poor.

With the gangs fighting for control of more turf and more money for the drug trade, the sale of drugs would come to a halt, unless the cartel came in and took it over. This could open the door for the cartels fighting it out in the cities where they do business. It would be the street gangs against the cartels trying to control the drugs coming in with the cartels. It would be a civil war with the gangs choosing sides of which cartel is going to give them a better deal. All of this started to sink into the team and all of them knew there would be a bloody outcome to whoever won the war. If the cartels won, the gangs would pay for their disobedience and if the gangs won, the cartel would be in a struggle for their fair share of the money coming from the sales until the cartel regained control again.

By now it was time for lunch and all the team was famished. They headed to the local café for lunch and more talking.

Buck pulled Rachael aside on the way out the door to the café. "Do you believe Jim could do all of this?"

Rachael stood there thinking for a moment, "I think he can with the right support."

"If this is the case, we need to find out who his source is. Do you have friends in the ATF who would be willing to assist us in finding any gun sales going on in Southern California?"

"As a matter of fact, I do know one of the agents working in the Southern California district."

With that, Buck and Rachael went back into the office, and Rachael placed a call to the ATF office in California.

As the phone was ringing, Rachael said, "Buck get me a pencil and a pad of paper to write on, just in case."

Buck complied and waited for the call to be finished.

When someone on the other end picked up the phone, Rachael identified herself to the person on the other end and asked, "Is Sue Johnson around?"

This time Rachael put it on speaker phone. When Sue answered the phone, Rachael identified herself again. "You still going out with Mike Chester, or was it Bill Tillman?"

Sue knew who it was immediately after the questions and started to laugh. "I had to drop them both; they wanted me to quit carrying a gun and go straight."

Rachael chuckled at this. "Without your gun who's going to protect you?"

They both laughed. When they quit laughing, Sue asked, "What can I do for you?"

Rachael told Sue what had been going on with the cartels and the Mafia and Jim.

With that, Rachael asked, "Is there anything you could tell us that might be going on with gun sales or shipments?"

"The word on the street is that something big is going down and it requires a lot of firepower to make it happen. Without getting into too many details over the phone you might want to come out and visit our office in the near future."

"Is there anything you can tell me that might help us on this end?"

"Just rumors at this point. Let me look into it and I'll send you an e-mail if anything bears fruit."

Rachael closed out the conversation. "I look forward to hearing from you."

With that, Buck and Rachael left for the café to eat.

# Chapter XII

Jim was watching the sun set in California on the Newport Beach pier. As he stood there watching, his mind was on his next step. He had already gotten rid of two mafia henchmen that had been tailing him when he went to California from Arizona. Pretending to want to meet the head guy of the Mafia was easy, especially when he showed them the money he was carrying with him. Being greedy has its own drawbacks, especially when it comes to thinking clearly. Jim smiled to himself about having to get rid of Hernandez and Martinez. They both looked surprised when he pulled his gun out and shot them. He knew their intentions were to do the same thing to him. Their deaths were necessary to start a war between the rival gang territories that they had driven through. No one in the Mafia knew about Jim yet, he had been very discreet about this part of his plan. The Mafia would think that the

Men of the Night or the Firebirds were involved with the killing of their people. An eye for an eye was the typical response in these cases; you kill one of ours, we kill two of yours. Jim couldn't help but laugh out loud for a moment. It had been too easy to start this war between the gangs, they were already suspicious of each other to start with. All it took was an opportunity to start the ball rolling. Jim had contacted his people about what he'd done and, of course, they were pleased with his actions. The next step was to take out the rival gang's own soldiers and make it look like retaliation from the Mafia. The two he chose were drug pushers with money and drugs on them. The hit was supposedly set up as a reprisal and robbery for what had happened to their gang. Now all he had to do was sit back and watch the fireworks. Jim had always liked working alone; however, in this case he had to depend on others to assist him in the gang war. He had always thought of himself as better than most of his contemporaries, and since having to deal with the loss of his wife, Karen, and giving up his son to continue the plan, he needed to leave New Rio behind.

Karen had been getting too lazy, wanting more and more from the embezzlement of the bank's laundered money. He tried to tell her not to go on spending sprees that would arouse suspicion from the locals they had met. But Karen refused to stop, thereby having new things was the standard process.

Karen had become a liability to the money-laundering operation. Jim's bosses were concerned about this and he knew something had to be done about it. He had loved Karen with all of her failings and their son was the most important thing to happen to him. When the bosses in Chicago told Jim that Karen had become a liability, he knew what that meant for him; he would be raising their son alone. Jim had no other recourse than to let the decision stand when it came to Karen. He had learned it could have been him as well when it came to liabilities.

Once the decision had been made, there was nothing he could do about it, Karen had to go and he was happy it wasn't him. The method of tying up loose ends was beyond his knowledge; he just knew it would be happening soon. Her greediness had been her downfall, and his need to survive for his son was paramount.

When the hit was put out by Chicago, Jim started thinking of a way to do in his former bosses for what they were going to do to Karen. Chicago had gotten complacent in the drug operations, and Jim knew that could be his way of getting back at them for Karen. All he had to do was find a way to destroy the trust Chicago had with their drug pushers. He knew that for this to work he would need more support from Chicago to come down and assist him in his apparent takeover of the gangs.

Jim had contacted the Monterrey Cartel to let them know of his actions and intentions. By letting them know, he could set up a trap for the Chicago group and destroy them. He would get even for what they had done to Karen, and he would have the last laugh. The cartel was, of course, leery about Jim's offer, but after he explained why, they agreed in principle to help him. The two Mafia henchmen were killed in order to protect his cover, a small price to pay for the bigger prize.

Jim was now beginning to feel cold from the wind blowing in from the ocean and was ready to go back to his hotel room. As he walked along the beach, the lights of the houses that lined the beach were on, and he could see people settling down to dinner and watching TV. He knew what he had to do for his Karen, and he would see it through for her. Tomorrow would be a meeting with some of the drug dealers and the heads of the local gangs. He would have his men from Chicago waiting in key places to ensure that the meeting was just a meeting. If it got ugly, they would be there to keep the peace. This was step two in his plan to get the gangs together to determine who would be in charge of the drug trade for Southern California. Then he would attack the weaker gang and set up the other gang as the ones who did the hit. That would start the war between the gangs and would place Chicago in a position to take over. Chicago would take over just in time to be taken out by the other gangs simultaneously. They would hit the Chicago gang in their own back yard and take out their dealers on the streets. Jim grinned when he thought about it, knowing that the hit would create a vacuum in the hierarchy of the Chicago group. At this point he reached his hotel room and went to bed as he knew it was going to be a busy day tomorrow.

# CHAPTER XIII

When Buck and Rachael got back to the office after eating, Rachael checked her e-mail account and found an e-mail waiting for her from Sue Johnson. As she read the e-mail, her eyes widened to let Buck know something had happened while they were eating. Buck looked at Rachael with a question on his face, and as he stood there, she started reading the e-mail out loud to Buck.

"Looked into your problem and found an arms shipment of automatic weapons making their way here and wasn't able to intercept them. The starting point seems to be from Chicago and is being escorted by Chicago personnel. All indications are that somebody is looking to start a war here in California. Will keep you updated."

After Rachael finished reading the e-mail out loud, she made sure the e-mail was sent to the rest of the team. It was for certain Jim was in California and that he was involved in this somehow.

Buck sat there for a moment. "And so it begins; what do we do from here?"

Rachael leaned back in her chair. "What are we supposed to do? All of the agencies have been notified and are aware that something is going down. The FBI and LAPD can handle it from there. All we can do is wait and see."

Evans came in and Rachael told him of the e-mail and what was happening.

"Our nightmare has taken a big step in the wrong direction. What we have been waiting for is about to start. I just hope none of the good guys get hurt," Evans replied.

The next morning Jim woke up to his phone ringing. Jim answered it already knowing who it was. He went down to the main hotel area where they served breakfast and began to eat. After finishing breakfast he got into his car and drove down to meet the Chicago people who were staying in another hotel. Jim knocked on the door to their hotel room and waited for the door to open. As he stood there, he looked around to make sure no one else knew he was there and that he wasn't followed. After a minute the door opened and there, standing in the doorway, stood a man wearing a suit with sunglasses. Once the man recognized Jim he let him into the room. Jim let his eyes acclimate to the darkness of the room. As he did so, he could discern that there were three men in the room besides himself, with a fourth man coming out of the bathroom holstering his gun. Once everyone was accounted for they turned on the light in the hotel room. By now Jim had a piece of paper lying out on the table in the room. Jim had drawn a layout of the area that the men and Jim were going to. On the paper you could see where he wanted each one of these men positioned for maximum cover.

"This," he exclaimed, "would give excellent firing positions in case the meeting goes bad."

The men in the room looked over the layout to make sure they knew where to be in position for the meeting.

With this all covered Jim asked, "Where is the hardware for this meeting?"

One of the men answered, "It's in the bags stashed in the lockers at the bus depot."

"Who you got watching the bus depot?" asked Jim.

The same man answered, "Two more guys sitting in the depot waiting for us."

Jim knew that the guns were to be used as an offering/enticement to the gangs they were meeting, with a promise of more coming if they played ball with Jim and his people. This weapon, which was now being introduced to the marines as a more reliable weapon than the M4, was the M27 Infantry Automatic Rifle (IAR). Very similar to the M4, the IAR can fire in fully automatic mode, while the standard M4 has single shot, semi-automatic and three-round burst options. The M27 costs about $3,000 dollars apiece, without the sight. The IAR would be considered the weapon of choice just for its ability to fire continuously. Jim had made certain that they only brought three of these to show the gangs, with the promise of more if they did what his organization wanted them to do. The IAR would be perfect against the police and other gangs that encroached into the IAR gang's territory. Jim had hoped this would bring the gangs of Southern California together, out in the open. Jim's meeting place was in neutral territory located in some old warehouses near the docks in Long Beach. The building was able to be protected from above, as well as from the front and back. The meeting would only have a few people from each gang who were in charge.

Arriving about an hour early to set up for the meeting, Jim placed his men in the areas already identified. Three of the men would be sitting in the rafters with rifles, watching from above. Another four would be watching from outside on each end of the street before leading to the main meeting place with radios and ear pieces to advise Jim of the outside situation. Jim hired two other local guys to stand with him when the gang leadership showed up. In all, there would be ten people for the meeting when the gangs came to meet. At 1:00 pm the first of the gangs showed, the Firebirds leadership, a predominately African-American street gang founded during the mid-1970s. As they met with Jim and his two people the gang spread itself out to protect its leader from whatever may happen. About ten minutes later the Rollin' Thunder gang came driving up. At first everybody started to get excited. Jim knew the Rollin Thunder's were the main rivals to the Firebirds and that their conflict went back to 1979. It was considered to be one of the biggest and most fierce rivalries between any two gangs in Southern California. Jim knew in order for his plan to work, he needed these two gangs to work together. Jim called on his radio and asked for a demonstration of the new IAR rifle.

When the shots rang out, he yelled to the leaders, "Now that I've got your attention,

I want to offer you a proposition that will benefit your organizations."

The two gang leaders put their hands up as a signal to have their people not fire on anybody.

Jim continued, "I need your help in setting up a new drug-distribution system in both of your areas."

Both of the gang leaders shook their heads no, and the guns came up pointing at Jim.

Jim looked down the barrels of the guns. "Before you kill me none of you will make it out of here alive unless I say so."

The Rollin Thunder's boss spoke, "What you want here in our territory? We don't need you stickin' your nose in our business."

The Firebirds leader agreed with him. "We don't need any whitey telling us how to do our job."

"How would you like to make a 100% increase in your profits selling drugs?" said Jim.

This got the gang leaders' attention.

"How would you like to increase your territory and control it?" Jim continued.

The gang leaders looked at each other and looked at Jim. "We can do that anytime we want. What makes you think you can help us do that?"

At this point Jim showed them the new IAR, "Fully automatic, no short bursts, will take out anything you want. I can supply your gangs with this with all of the ammo you need."

Both gang leaders looked at the rifle, both of them thinking what they could do with this new weapon if they had it. Then Jim went to the back of his car and opened the trunk and pulled out two RPGs for them as well.

"I don't think you will have many problems with the police, either, with this. Go ahead, keep it"

This got the attention of the gang leaders. One of them said, "Man where did you get that?"

"Doesn't matter; all you need to know is I can supply you with as many as you want."

Both the gang leaders were now saying, "What's in it for you?"

"Just like I said, I want to supply you with drugs and you in return give me the money from the sales."

"What about the Mafia, I don't think they'll appreciate us or you taking over," said the Firebirds leader.

Jim tossed the RPG to the one gang leader. "I don't see a problem do you?"

The gang leaders smiled at this and shook their heads no.

Jim continued, "The first shipment of drugs will come in two weeks from today. All I need you to do is wait till we deliver the drugs and use your network to sell it. I or one of my associates will be by to collect the money and deliver more drugs. By doing business with us you will see a 10% increase in profits for yourselves." Both gang leaders looked at each other and before they could say anything Jim said, "Before you ask why I need the other gang to sell the drugs, ask yourself this, who is your competitor in California?"

The gang leaders looked at each other.

"I think you already know the answer. What my organization wants to do is expand all across the USA from the west to the east coast. Your gangs are the toughest and the most diversified throughout the west and Rocky Mountain region. We want to expand your horizons in this endeavor. That being said, we need both of your gangs to do this. You're going to learn how to play nice with each other from now on," Jim said.

Both of the leaders looked at each other and said, "If the price is right, we can get along with anybody."

The gang leaders laughed at this.

"Do we have a deal?" Jim asked.

"Yes, but if you double-cross us in any way, we will kill you and your people, comprende, whitey?"

Jim knew they meant business and was not taking their threats lightly. As they drove away from the meeting, the first step was in place; now it was time to deliver the goods.

Jim used his radio and called to the teams at the end of the building, "Follow them a short distance and take out one of the gang leaders and make it look like the other gang did it."

The team followed in their car and waited for the right time to hit the Rollin' Thunder's gang leader. While the Rollin' Thunder's leader was sitting at a stoplight, an RPG round hit the SUV he was sitting in. The blast lifted the SUV about ten feet into the air. It came back down on top of another car. The fire from the RPG detonated the gas tank of the SUV to finish it off. The car the SUV landed on caught fire as well; fortunately, the people inside were able to get out with minor burns. As Jim saw the black smoke in the sky, he smiled and thought to himself, so it begins. Jim showed up at the burning SUV, walked over to it and pulled anything he could find that would identify it as being the Rollin Thunder gang. The leader of the Rollin Thunder gang never knew what hit him, by the time he realized what had happened, he was burned beyond recognition. The driver survived the blast only because his window was down, and although it burned over 50 % of his body, was able to crawl out. The driver would spread the word about the gang leader having an RPG given to him. Jim packed up his team and drove them to their cars and dropped them off. At this time Jim drove to his own hotel room and changed clothes to go swimming in the pool. Jim smiled, knowing that the RPG he left with the Firebirds would be blamed for the Rollin Thunder leader's demise. By now the team that did the hit was on their way back to Chicago and would be reading about it in the newspaper the next day. With this hit Jim knew the gang war was about to begin and he would be there to pick up the pieces.

# CHAPTER XIV

When the news of the gang hit had been televised, Rachael received a phone call from Sue at ATF informing her about the hit. Rachael stood there listening to Sue in a state of shock. In broad daylight using a very powerful weapon in the city was ballsy, to say the least! She wondered who would be so willing to do something like this. Was it a gang hit like everybody was saying, or was it something else? She thanked Sue for the information and asked to keep her in the loop with anything they found. Buck walked in and saw the look on Rachael's face.

"What happened?"

"There was a gang hit in Southern California; one of the leaders of one of the most powerful gangs in the area was just taken out in broad daylight."

Foster and Evans came through the door to the office and saw both Buck and Rachael looking bewildered.

Sensing something was wrong, Evans asked, "Has it already started?"

Rachael apprised them both of the phone call from ATF and what she knew of the gang hit. Not wanting to believe it was more than a gang hit, Foster started checking his sources once again.

Jeff and Wendy knew the implications the gangland hit would have on the other gangs in the Southern California area, as did Linda. They all knew that a gang war was about to start, and LAPD was in it for the long haul. They realized that other police departments would be involved as well. It would take all of their resources to control or contain the fallout from this war. The state and county would be in on it, trying to stop all-out bloodshed. The FBI would give the police all their resources for Intel, as would every federal agency. The war on the ground would be fought mainly by the local police agencies that were considered to be the foot soldiers in the trenches. They would determine who would win the war in the gang's territory.

Jeff and Wendy would advise their counterparts in DEA about the gang hit. DEA could track the drugs as to who was getting them from the cartel. Maybe they could find out who was trying to take over the business. Linda was already working out the angles of which gangs were to benefit or lose from this war.

With the other gangs watching from the sidelines, some of them would join with whoever stood to pay out the most in their behalf. Others would sit it out and pick up the pieces of what was left from the fight and then make their move to expand or consolidate their territory. Not unlike the vultures waiting for the death of an animal so that they could feast on the carcasses. From the looks of it the battle wouldn't take too long. It was always a matter of time for the victor to rise above the carnage created by the war. The others would follow suit to pay homage to the victors and destroy the losers as if they had never existed. Some would call this the circle of life gang-style in the cities. Eventually, others would fill the void left by the losers;

however, that would take time to happen, how much time depended on the amount of money there was to make. Then, when the smoke cleared from the war, it would be business as usual in the city. The ripple effect of the war would be felt all the way back to the cartels who were the suppliers of the drug. The cartels' main concern was the distribution of drugs and the money coming back to them from the sale of the drugs. Who delivered and who died in the process was not their concern, unless it stopped the flow of money and the drugs.

The cartels had their own problems with the locals in Mexico; what happened on American soil was not their main concern. The people they had to contend with were the Mexicans who would stand up against the cartels in their own country. It always seemed that somebody was opposed to the selling of drugs and, of course, they had to be killed or disappear never to be heard from again. The cartels were used to the fighting in the drug wars. The cartels fought amongst themselves all of the time; to them it was business as usual. Life and death meant nothing in the drug world, unless it was you that died. A man named Stalin once said: You kill one person, that is murder; you kill twenty people or maybe a hundred, that is considered a massacre; and you kill thousands or millions, that is a statistic. At this point the people dying from the drug war are just statistics, names without faces or lives that most people don't care about because it's too hard to comprehend. The lives lost in the drug wars were of no consequence to the users or to the ones that would kill or rob to get their fix.

As Jim was sitting poolside his phone rang. He answered and the voice on the other end said, "Team two is in position."

"Proceed," Jim responded.

He calmly put the phone down and continued sleeping on the lounge. The voice on the other end of the phone proceeded to tell his team, "It's a go."

The team started setting up their equipment for the next phase of the operation. The two shooters pulled out their 50 caliber rifles cases. Both of the shooters get

onto their ATVs and drove in two different directions. The first sniper headed further up the highway and threaded his way
onto the peak overlooking the road and
uncased his sniper rifle and started setting
it up. The second shooter was on the same
side as the team but parallel to the shooter
on the opposite side of the road. He
opened the case to his rifle and attached
the silencer to the barrel of his weapon
and, once set up, waited for the signal.
Both snipers had ear wigs for communica-
tion to the team lead and to notify the
leader when they were set and ready.

The team lead looked at his watch and
saw that it was 2:30 in the afternoon and
told the shooters to stand by. At approximately 2:45 pm he started scanning the
highway with his binoculars. Finally, he
saw a car coming down the road and
started following it, he whispered into the
radio mike, "Stand by." The two shooters
started looking down the highway towards the oncoming car. The leader sent
another message to the road crew working
on the highway and gave them the go

code. The leader was now looking for the drug car and the chase car, knowing that they would be making their entrance soon. The flagman, who was wearing an orange vest with a stop sign, signaled for the car to slow down. The other guys working the road started spreading dirt and gravel on the highway. When the car stopped the flagman had his sign showing stop.

The driver of the car rolled down his window. "How long is it going to be before we can move again?"

"Just a couple of minutes; they're just starting to clean up the job."

The flagman talked into his radio, "Go ahead."

The first shot from the sniper on the other side of the highway took out the engine on the car. The driver looked at his gauges and couldn't figure out what happened to his car. The drug car was now coming down the road from the same direction as the first car.

The leader spoke into the microphone. "On their way."

The second sniper was lining up on the car carrying the drugs. Once the drug car slowed down the second sniper took out the driver with a head shot. The bullet tore through the top of the car into the driver's head; the blood spray from the shot hit the inside of the windshield, covering it. The flagman pulled out a small Uzi and sprayed the occupants in the first car. He calmly walked over to the drug car and did the same to the occupants in that car also. At this time the road crew brought out a heavy-duty forklift and picked up the car and drove it to the side of the road and pushed the first car off into the ravine. The second car with the drugs was opened up by two of the road crew, and the drugs and money were transferred to a work truck and hid inside the panels of the door. The forklift driver took the second car and pushed it down into the same ravine. By this time the road crew went back to working on the highway and the flagman waved the chase car down and, after a couple of minutes sitting, there allowed the car to proceed on down the highway.

Once the chase car was out of sight, the team made their way back to the base camp where the leader was and started tearing down all of their equipment. The team and their equipment were loaded into the trucks hauling the forklift and ATV trailers back to Phoenix.

Jim received another call, "All's good."

"Bring the drugs to me and I'll take care of the rest."

Jim put the phone down and decided he'd had enough sun for the day and headed back to his room. As he was walking back to his room he looked at his watch and saw that it was 3:30 Arizona time and 2:30 California time and decides he'd have an early dinner, after all.

By now Jeff, Wendy, and Linda were working their resources to try and find out who was behind the gang hit. There was nothing definite as to who did it; the survivor wasn't talking or couldn't talk because of the burns all over his body. He was induced into a medical coma to ease his pain and to start the healing process. His chances for survival were pretty good, although it would take some time for the process to work. All the Rollin' Thunder gang lieutenants had been to see the driver, all of them trying to figure out what had happened, to no avail. They knew of the meeting but couldn't piece together this outcome. The questions now on their minds were who did it and what to do about it. The death of the gang leader sent shock waves throughout the gang and their competitors. What was the gang going to do for retribution? All of them were looking for the people/gang who would have done this. The question that remained was why? Was it for control of new territory, or was it for a bigger piece of the pie? As far the gang was concerned, it was eye for an eye, body for body, blood for blood. Just who would do something this bold to their leader? Was it the Brass Ravens, Men of the Night, Firebirds, or the Ebony Cobras? As far as the Rollin Thunders were concerned, each had their own motive to try this. All they knew for sure was somebody was going to pay for it. It was just a matter of time before the driver would come out of the coma and say what happened. Every gang in the area was suspect, even the ones who claimed they were innocent. For now the Rollin' Thunders were sitting tight, waiting for the chance for payback.

Jim was up early the next morning, getting ready to leave. He had paid his hotel bill the night before. He loaded his suitcase into the car and closed the trunk. Then he went back to the room to do a final check. That done, he drove out of the hotel parking lot and headed towards Phoenix to pick up the drugs. By now Jim knew the cartel was missing their drugs and there would be hell to pay if and when they caught up with the thieves who stole it. Jim had made an agreement that he would return the drugs to the cartel once he got them, that being said, he had changed his mind. Jim knew the Chicago group would be blamed for the theft of the drugs and the murders of the Mafia as well. He wanted this to happen; the Chicago group would pay dearly for what they had done to Karen. He smiled to himself, knowing that his life would be worthless if caught by any of the groups. Putting that thought aside, his first step was to retrieve the drugs and head back to New Rio and wait for the next act to play itself out. Hiding in plain sight would be hard to do.

"Steady, Jim, he told himself, first things first, getting the drugs in Phoenix and the next step in California."

Arriving in Phoenix to retrieve the drugs was the first thing to be done. After contacting the team leader, Jim set up a pickup point somewhere around Mesa, near the Arizona State University campus. With the kids walking around the area strangers wouldn't stand out as much. Finding the right place was easy; there was an indoor parking lot used by the public. Using the third level and deep inside the building would keep prying eyes from seeing the tradeoff.

With the drugs in tow and the team paid for their services, Jim left to go back to California to sell the drugs to the pushers. The five-hour return trip to California was uneventful and, in fact, quite boring. When he returned to Los Angeles, he contacted the leaders of the gangs in order to set up a meet. Jim knew this meeting probably wouldn't go as smooth as the first time. In the meantime Jim was basically a tourist seeing Sea World, Disneyland, and Universal Studios all of the places he and Karen visited when they were first married. Jim went there to remember the good times with Karen and the fun they had going out to dinner at night, buying stuffed animals at Disneyland, getting wet on the log plume ride, sweet memories during good times. Jim started to cry a little but regained his composure after a minute or two. His only thought was getting even with the people who had killed his Karen, this brought a smile to his lips.

After two days of playing tourist Jim received a phone call from his team, who had arrived by plane earlier that day.

"Same setup as before in the first meeting; however, be ready for the idiots to be jumpy. After we took out the gang leader they should be nervous, and I'm sure they'll bring an army for this visit," Jim explained.

The man on the other end of the phone asked, "Should we prepare for a war?"

"I'm thinking so," Jim replied.

"We'll bring the hardware for the visit," The voice said.

"Good."

Jim didn't want to take any chances with the gangs. He knew they would be on edge; the lure of easy money would bring the gangs back to the meeting place. What happened from there was anybody's guess. He knew to be prepared. This time he would be armed as well with his own gun, a Kimber 1911 45 ACP. The first time he picked it up it felt like a hand in a glove, just right. From that point on, the Kimber was always with him and always ready to use.

Jim drove to the meeting site an hour early to survey the layout one more time and to reassure himself that all was ready. The rest of the team would show up in about a half hour. This time the team would have RPGs at the ready, along with automatic rifles and flashbangs to keep everybody off guard. Jim did not want to use the firepower; this was all about being safe for himself and his team. The goal here is to sell the drugs and get the money to the cartel. The Mafia would be involved only as Jim would allow. The goal was for the gangs to fight it out for the control of the drug trade. The Mafia had no clue who stole their drugs and where it would end up. When the local gangs would sell it on the street, the markings on the kilos would let the Mafia know who took the drugs and killed their couriers. This would begin a war between the couriers and street gangs that would hopefully bury both the Mafia and gangs in Southern California.

When the team showed up, Jim had already examined the entrance to the meet and the exit from the meet and had the team set up accordingly. The RPGs had better use in the exit side of the area. The automatic rifles and snipers would oversee the meet and be at the entrance hidden in the shadows of the surrounding buildings. The flashbangs would be held by Jim and another member of the team, who would be with Jim when the meet took place. This would surprise the gangs and give Jim and his bodyguard time to use their weapons if the need arose. Everything was set 30 minutes before the gangs showed up, and now it was a waiting game. The meet was to take place at 3:00 and in the heat of the day Jim was starting to sweat.

At five minutes past 3:00 the SUVs started to appear. The first to appear was the Rollin' Thunder gang, and their army was in the second SUV. In another ten minutes the Firebirds appeared in their Cadillac cars. They parked away from the Rollin' Thunders and set up their army as a defense against the other gang. Jim stepped out of the shadow of the building and waved at both gang leaders to come over to where he was.

Jim yelled out to the gangs as they were making their way over to him, "Just the leaders, no one else."

At first the leaders stopped and looked around to make sure it was safe to proceed. The armies on both sides didn't like this at all, so to enforce what he wanted Jim signaled to fire for effect in front of the gangs. The sound of the automatics opening up stopped the two armies from moving forward. The gang leaders just stood there a moment, and Jim stated again.

"Just the leaders, no one else."

The leaders of the gangs came forward and met Jim, both eyeing him and each other for any movement that would give away their intentions.

"Do you have the money?" Jim asked.

"Do you have the drugs?" The leaders asked.

Jim looked over at his bodyguard and nodded for him to get the two satchels of drugs. The body guard brought them out of the building and opened the satchels to show them. The leaders signaled to one of their men to bring the money.

"Do you want to check the drugs for purity?" Jim asked.

"No problem, whitey; if it's not we'll find you," both leaders said.

By then the two men carrying the money arrived and threw down the sacks of money.

This time the leaders asked, "Do you want to check it for the right amount you agreed to?"

Jim smile. "No, that won't be necessary I trust you."

At this they all laughed and gathered up the drugs and money and walked away.

Jim called out, "Same time, same place next month."

The leaders waved and their army of men moved into their separate vehicles and drove away. Jim was relieved that it went off without a hitch. Not only that, but he had the money to give to the cartel. Everything was working according to plan.

Evans and Foster were the first to hear about the theft of the drugs from the Mafia. They figured that 50 kilos had been taken by an unknown group of people.

This information had come from Jeff Call and Wendy Chu.

The cartel was up in arms as to who had done this. Needless to say, they were used to losing drugs to the local police and even ICE, but to lose the drugs and the drivers all at the same time was unheard of. No trace of the people or the drugs could be found. At first the cartel thought the Mafia had done it; however, there was no proof they were involved with it. The men in the chase car were questioned, under threat of death, denying they knew where the drugs were. The cartel didn't suffer fools well and shot them anyway to make a point about the theft of the drugs. Jeff and Wendy had heard through the Intel network that the Monterrey Cartel was now looking at other cartels, thinking they were trying to take over their business.

When Buck, Rachael and Linda reported into the office, they were briefed as to what the DEA Intel had heard. Linda had also wanted to brief the team about the gangland hit in Southern California. The residue from the blast proved it had been an

RPG that had taken out the SUV and the Rollin' Thunder's gang leader.

"This was the first time a hit had been done in broad daylight and the first time anything bigger than guns was used for the hit," Linda said.

Everybody knew about RPGs and how effective they could be, but up to this point none had ever been used on U.S. soil. The FBI was interested in finding out where the RPG came from and if there were more out there. The ATF, with Sue as point of contact, would furnish the team with information as needed. All anybody could say at this point was somebody was playing hardball with the drug business and they didn't care about the body count.

The team knew bad things were going down; the why and who of it was the proverbial thorn in their side. Was this Jim or some other group; no one knew for certain. Again, what was certain was they needed to find Jim and figure out if he was behind all of this.

Buck and Rachael drove back to the cave where they found the mules carrying the drugs. In the daylight they might find something that might prove useful. Evans and Foster were checking the latest Intel for any signs as to who had done this. The gangs in Southern California were still delivering the drugs to the streets. According to the police departments, you could feel the tension in the air, especially on the street corners where the dealers met with their customers. The dealers were carrying guns, looking for the people not supposed to be there. With everyone on edge the chances of something stupid happening was magnified greatly. All of the dealers knew they could be the next ones to be hit by an unknown group or persons carrying RPGs.

The Rollin' Thunders were blaming the Firebirds for the hit on their boss, especially now that the driver was conscious and detailed his story about what looked like a rocket coming towards them from behind. The trust factor was at an all-time low for being business partners. The Rollin' Thunders couldn't and wouldn't let this ride; as it is in prison, you show any sign of weakness, everybody then tries to take you out. It is the same on the streets, like ravenous dogs turning on the weak one in the pack. There's no room for the weak ones anywhere or anytime. The waterfall effect would begin until the Rollin' Thunders paid back whoever it was that took out their boss. With this in mind, the Rollin' Thunders started planning their payback. Maybe the next meet with Jim, who was giving them the drugs, would be the time and place for the hit. Besides, why share the profits when you can have it all for yourself. Maybe the Rollin' Thunders would hopefully come out on top and with more territory than before. Right now the main thing the Rollin' Thunders needed was a break that would help them solve the question as to who took out their boss.

# Chapter XV

As they made their way to the cave, both Buck and Rachael knew they were looking for the proverbial needle in the haystack; the chances of finding anything in the cave would be a miracle. When Rachael lit the lantern she was carrying, the light of the lantern made everything in the cave look different. The shadows caused by the light made it look as if they were in a monster movie from the 1940s like the "Mummy." This made Rachael cling to Buck by grabbing his arm and hanging onto it. Buck didn't mind this at all; in fact, as they were searching the cave, he spooked her a couple of times which made her scream a little each time. He would laugh and she would hit him, scolding him for doing it. The cave went back into the mountain about 50 feet and got bigger the deeper they went. When they reached the end of the cave, they realized that there was nothing of value in the cave; it was a long shot that didn't pay out.

Buck looked at Rachael. "You look stunning in this light."

"Now who's the romantic, and in a cave no less."

Buck looked at her and kissed her long and hard and let her go.

"Your timing is a little off. Here we are in a cave where bodies have been found and now you want to get romantic?" Rachael said.

"I didn't want to lose my courage. Besides, with the satellites above, they would have caught us, and I'm sure there could have been a state department issue with the Russians watching," Buck smiled.

"You think of everything don't you?" Rachael laughed.

They made their way out of the cave back into the sunlight and with nothing to show for their trip and headed back to town.

While in the truck Buck said, "Supposing Jim wasn't involved with killing the four in the cave, supposing he had nothing to do with any of this?"

Rachael looked at him, questioning his thoughts. "I'm listening."

"Maybe they're not connected at all with Jim? Granted it wasn't random that the Mexicans were killed. But who would stand to gain if these murders occurred and the drugs they were carrying were taken from them? Which begs the question, where could you sell the drugs around here without raising suspicion?"

Rachael thought on this. "The pawn-shop owner possibly, maybe. He would have the money and maybe the connections to sell it, thereby making a profit without raising any suspicion."

"Who would he sell it to?"

"Who has that kind of money in town?"

Buck thought on this one for a moment. "Somebody who has access to money or maybe somebody who is well off. Most likely someone who is above suspicion and capable of transporting the drugs where they need to go to sell."

"Is there anybody like that in town? Someone who is greedy and doesn't have a problem with killing to get gain, and knows the area like you do?"

"The only one that fits that bill would be our county sheriff, who used to live here as a kid. He's about 20 years older than I am. But he grew up here and was quite the explorer. He works at the county seat, which is about 60 miles from here. If anybody knows anything, it would be him."

"Do you think he would be able to do something like what we saw in the cave?"

"I don't know him well enough to hazard a guess on that. But he has the connections and the wherewithal to do it."

When Buck and Rachael got back to the office, they floated their thought to both Foster and Evans on the county sheriff. Evans looked at Foster and asked what he thought about it.

"There have been rumors about the county sheriff being dirty for years. No one has been able to prove anything, and every time we try to set up a sting our cover is blown before we get anything accomplished," Foster replied.

Foster continued, "We know that there are flights coming in at night landing in the desert, delivering marijuana and other stuff, but by the time we get there the plane is gone and so are the drugs. Knowing the sheriff, I wouldn't be surprised if he was involved."

"How do we prove it?" Evans said.

"That's easy, I've been keeping him in the loop ever since we started this investigation. I could feed him some information that might bring him out in the light."

"There is a story about the sheriff being involved in a fight with a teenager at a local burger place, where the teenager was getting the better of him. He supposedly grabbed the kid by the neck and stuck his face into the deep fryer in the kitchen. The kid swore afterwards he was going to kill him for what he had done to him. Nobody knows whatever happened to the kid after that," Buck stated.

Everybody winced after hearing the story, knowing how it would have hurt to have that happen to them.

"I wouldn't put it past him to have done that; he seems like he has his own agenda for things happening in this county. Needless to say, we need to look at him for any and all connections in this mess," Foster said.

"Where do we start?" Evans asked.

"How about we claim that we found evidence that proves that Jim had nothing to do with this murder and that it points to a local law enforcement official in New Rio. If the sheriff contacts us about this new information, which he will, we may get him to bite on it," Foster said.

"We need to plant some evidence that only he would know about and know where to look for it." Evans said.

"How about something that was found on our second trip out there?" said Rachael.

"You could call the sheriff with an update about what we found out there," Buck said, looking at Foster.

"How about we use a signed confession from someone that survived and just came forward since the shooting and is willing to testify identifying the murderer as a county deputy?" said Rachael.

Buck looked around. "Where are we going to keep this somebody and who is it going to be?"

First of all, it has to be somebody he wouldn't recognize and it has to be in town in a safe house for protection," replied Foster.

"The county sheriff would know me and Buck, so we're out of the loop. How about a girl who he has never seen, someone who looks like they have been hiding and who is from old Mexico with her clothes torn and dirty?"

They all looked at Rachael.

"Can you do the part of the woman from old Mexico?" Foster asked.

Rachael looked around at the men. "I can do it better than any of you ugly guys can," she said smiling. "I just won't wear any makeup when I do this."

Buck rolled his eyes. "If that doesn't work, we will keep the lights down low."

Everybody laughed at this and Rachael looked surprised at Buck and pretended to be shot in the heart.

Buck walked over to her. "Are you sure you want to do this?"

Rachael looked at him. "There is nothing worse than a dirty cop, and with you as my backup I feel pretty safe about this."

"I love you and don't want to lose you over a dirty cop."

Rachael looked into his eyes. "I love you too, and you won't if you're there to protect me from him."

They both felt that this was something that had to be done, no matter the outcome.

"We need a safe place to put her while she's supposedly waiting to file her statement with the FBI. Where do you suggest, Buck?" Foster said.

Buck thought a moment and suggested, "A hotel room on the outskirts of New Rio."

"Can we protect her there in the hotel room?" asked Evans.

Foster thought for a moment, "We set up surveillance cameras inside the room with audio equipment and watch from the adjoining room. We'll need to leave the doors unlocked that lead to the main room where she'll be."

All agreed that this would be the place for the trap. Foster directed the team to make Rachael ready for her role. Evans and Foster would send a message informing the sheriff that they found a survivor of the shooting in the cave. Buck looked at Rachael, and in his eyes he said, "Good luck." She returned his look with "Don't screw this up" in her eyes.

The next day Rachael was ready for her role as the Mexican maiden found in the desert by Buck. She was to be considered bedridden from being out in the desert heat without water. The stage would be set up for Rachael to be monitored by a nurse in the room with an IV bottle hooked to her arm to replenish her for hydration. The nurse would be Linda from the FBI, who would be there the whole time. Rachael would lie in bed in a catatonic state, waiting to gain enough strength to make a statement to the FBI and state police. The state police would have a trooper outside her hotel room door, standing guard and making sure no one got through without his permission. The other adjoining rooms would be wired for sound and video, with Foster and Evans in one room monitoring all that took place, and the other room would be filled with state troopers watching as well. Buck would be in the bathroom hiding in the dark, watching and listening to all that was going on in the main room. Fortunately, the room being guarded was on the second floor and was inside the main part of the building. All doors would be closed off with the exception of the door leading into the room where Rachael would be. All of the players were wearing ear wigs to monitor the conversation as it played out and waiting for the signal to go in at Foster's command. All was in place by noon and everybody knew their part, the message had been sent to the sheriff. Foster was waiting to hear from the troopers, who were watching the roads leading into New Rio. If it all proved true, the waiting wouldn't take long for the sheriff to appear.

As the time moved slowly on, Foster and Evans were talking about what they were going to do after the investigation was done. Foster wanted to go fishing and Evans wanted to go back to the city to view the tall buildings and get lost in the city. Rachael who was lying in the bed was starting to get restless and wanted to move around a little bit. She put her gun on the nightstand and moved around the room to stretch a little.

About 6:00 pm Foster got the word that a county patrol car was inbound from the other side of town. Foster got up and went to the police station to meet the sheriff and let him know where they had the Mexican girl staying. When the county car showed up, it wasn't the sheriff inside the car; it was a county lieutenant deputy from the main office who got out of the car. Foster shook hands with the deputy and basically told the deputy what was going on since they found the girl. He explained she was resting comfortably in a safe house with a nurse watching over her and in a couple of days she would be ready to sign a statement about what she had seen.

Foster looked at the deputy and asked, "Why didn't the sheriff come down?"

"The sheriff was busy and asked me to come instead. Can I see the girl?"

Foster said, "Of course," and opened the door to take him to the hotel. They drove in Foster's car and parked outside the entrance to the hotel. Passing the front desk going to the elevator, Foster pushed the button for the elevator. They entered the elevator and went to the second floor. They exited the elevator and walked down the hall towards the trooper guarding the door and walked in. There on the bed lay the girl who had been found in the desert, with the nurse taking her blood pressure. Once done she looked at Foster and shook her head in the affirmative. Foster looked pleased to see that the girl was going to recover.

He looked at the deputy. "Looks like tomorrow she may be able to talk to us, God willing and if the rivers don't rise."

The deputy looked around the room, noticing that it was just the nurse in the room with the guard outside the door.

"Foster, it looks as if everything is good to go for her safety," he stated.

"The only ones that know she's here are you, me, the nurse, and the guard outside the door."

"Oh yeah, I almost forgot about him."

"He will be replaced by another trooper around 9:00 pm." Foster said.

With that, they left the room and headed down to the elevator to their car.

After taking the deputy back to the office Foster asked, "Are you hungry; I know a good café down the street."

The deputy begged of. "I need to get back to my office to report to the sheriff about this."

They shook hands and Foster said, "Once we get the report from the girl, we will send a copy of it to the sheriff."

"That would be fine."

With that, Foster headed towards the café to get something to eat. The deputy looked at Foster as he went into the café and went into the sheriff's office to make a phone call. Once inside, he called the sheriff directly and apprised him of the girl and where they were keeping her.

"Is it going to be a problem taking care of the girl?" The sheriff asked.

"The security around the room was nothing short of missing and now knowing where she is, it shouldn't be a problem."

"Good, you know what you need to do."

"It will be taken care of," and the deputy hung up the phone. With that he went to his car and drove off.

At this point Jeff and Wendy came out from behind a closed door and called Foster saying, "He took the bait. It looks as if the sheriff is in on it as well."

"Did you record it?" Foster asked.

Wendy, holding the tape, nodded her head yes.

"We got it," Jeff said.

Jeff hung up the phone and both Jeff and Wendy went out to the café for dinner and to drop off the tape recording.

With that done, Foster went back to the hotel and talked to Evans, "We have them on tape."

Evans was relieved and yet upset by this new information. He looked at Foster, shaking his head in bewilderment and anger.

"Here we are fighting an enemy more treacherous than any army we've ever encountered, and the people we put our trust in are the very murderers we are fighting against, and for what? Is their pay not 30 pieces of silver but thousands of dollars to be used for a more comfortable life for themselves? At the cost of what is morally right for all involved!"

Foster stood there, listening, "All things have a price, even freedom. The question is what are you willing to pay or take for the comforts of life, for security, and for a clear conscience?"

"Let's ask the people who have died at the hands of the cartels in Mexico, all 120,000 of them."

Everybody with the ear wigs heard the conversation between Evans and Foster, and all knew what the cost was for their freedom and pain for that freedom. With that, all went quiet and the rest of the evening was just waiting for the inevitable attempt on Rachael's life.

At about 8:30 the deputy was surveying the outside of the hotel, looking for any sign that would be a clue to call off the hit. Seeing none, he cautiously made his way to the door of the hotel. Dressed in regular street clothes, he fit in with the others milling about trying to get a room for the night. Once past the desk, he made his way to the stairwell that would lead him up to the second floor. The deputy opened the emergency fire door just an inch to verify that the trooper was still there guarding the door. Once confirmed, he went to the third floor and walked out onto the roof of the hotel. He had with him a rope to use to climb down to the second floor. The patio was small but big enough to land on without hurting yourself. The deputy looked inside and saw the nurse reading a magazine while the Mexican girl was still lying motionless on the bed. Foster knew the time was right for the hit to take place; the question was how would he do it?

A trooper watching the back side of the hotel called through the ear wig and said we have movement coming in on the patio. With that, everybody was ready. Buck tightened his grip on his semi-auto, waiting for the word. The nurse kept reading her magazine but put her free hand down into the cushions for her gun, and Rachael slipped the safety off of her weapon. Evans went to the patio window and tried to see who it was on the patio next to him. The trooper who had reported the movement sent another message saying that someone was opening the sliding window. With that, Evans went quietly outside onto his patio and waited for any movement coming from the hotel room. At this point Foster called for the team go in and stop the intruder. With guns drawn and people rushing from the side rooms into the main room, the deputy froze in place and for a second didn't know what to do. The deputy tried to go back the way he came in but was blocked by Evans with his gun drawn. The deputy was caught and quickly raised his hands in the air. Evans reached him first and grabbed the gun from his hand, slammed him to the floor while reading him his rights. Buck was standing next to Evans and looked at the deputy and hit him square in the jaw. Nobody stopped Buck from doing this; they all understood why. Buck walked over to Rachael. He saw that she was okay and then headed outside to get some air.

Foster was pleased when he got to the deputy. "Have you anything to say right now?"

"No."

"You'll have plenty to say later, I bet." Foster laughed.

Evans grabbed Foster. 'I've got an idea."

As Foster listened to Evans he started laughing. "It's worth a try; let's do it."

Foster and Evans went over to the deputy. "We need to have you call your boss and let him know the hit was good, but you need him to come down and take a look at what you found as far as new evidence from the cave."

"And if I don't?"

Foster looked at him. "Do you want to go down for the four murders all by yourself? Besides, we have you on tape talking to the sheriff earlier tonight."

"Maximum security prison, ex-policeman, death sentence, or maybe life; either way you are going to be miserable. You choose what you want," Evans piped in.

"I would sure as hell not go down by myself in this mess you helped create. Besides, he who tells his side of the story first will get the best deal there is, whatever it may be," Foster added.

The deputy thought about this for a moment. "I'll do it."

About 9:30 the county sheriff got the phone call from the deputy saying the hit was done. However, in his searching at the station he found some new evidence that could implicate the sheriff with the murders.

"Can you destroy it?" The sheriff asked.

"No, it's been cataloged into the FBI's system; if it comes up missing, someone will know about it from the records. I think you need to come down and take a look at it. Then you can decide what to do," the deputy replied.

The sheriff thought about it for a moment. "I'll be down in about an hour."

"I'll be waiting for you at the station."

Foster went and got Buck and told him of their plan.

All Buck could say was, "I want to be a part of it."

Rachael had cleaned herself up and was back into regular clothes again. She met Buck at the station and listened to the plan Foster and Evans played out with the deputy bringing the county sheriff down. Buck was going to be here to meet the county sheriff and show him the new evidence he had found at the cave.

Foster looked at Rachael. "You are going to show it to him because it belongs to the FBI and you're responsible for it. Buck, you will back up Rachael as needed and let it play out."

"Most likely he will try to take it by force. Let him take it and we'll take care of the rest. Just don't get shot; so far we're batting a thousand on that part of it," Evans said.

Foster grabbed the deputy and instructed him on what to do. "First of all, you will be waiting inside the office talking to Buck and Rachael as if nothing is wrong." Foster continued, "Second, you will show the evidence to the sheriff and ask what he wants to do with it. You will need to be in uniform as well. You will have your sidearm but it will be unloaded."

"If you're lucky you may not get shot when this goes down," Rachael said.

Buck looked at him. "I wouldn't bet on that."

The deputy started to turn white as a sheet at Buck's statement. Evans came in with some doctored evidence and placed it inside the holding room and marked it accordingly. The evidence they had was photos of the crime scene and of footprints to and from the cave. The most damming evidence was a county sheriff's badge and papers with the name of the county sheriff on it that they claimed they had found inside the cave. All of this was sealed inside a large manila envelope inside the holding room.

"You saw Rachael and Buck load it into the envelope when they did their cataloging of the evidence. That's why you needed the sheriff to come down and look into it for himself," Foster told the deputy.

"Oh, by the way, if you screw this up I'll make sure you're the first one shot," said Buck.

Evans looked at the deputy. "And we'll say you shot first."

With that in mind, everybody but Buck and Rachael left. They were not that far away but out of sight. With Buck getting the deputy a cup of coffee, they waited for the sheriff to show up. As the lights of the patrol car showed, Foster called ahead to let them know the sheriff was on his way.

Buck looked at the deputy. "Your life or his; you decide."

With that, Buck sat back down and waited for the door to open. When the county sheriff walked through the door, both the deputy and Buck stood up. Buck shook hands with the sheriff and offered him a cup of coffee. Rachael came over with the coffee and introduced herself to the sheriff as an FBI consultant on the robbery/murder case.

After a couple minutes of asking how the drive was, the sheriff asked, "I've heard there was new information or new evidence found dealing with the murders of the four Mexicans in the cave."

"Yes, that's true. Buck and I went back out and did another search of the cave and surrounding area and not only found a witness who had seen the whole thing, but also found some stuff that is pretty damming and could have repercussions for the county."

"That's the reason I called you," The deputy said.

"Would you like to see what we have as evidence?" Rachael asked.

"Yes, I would be very interested in seeing what you have."

Buck got up and went to the holding room to the filing cabinet and pulled the manila envelope and handed it to Rachael. After signing the property log she opened the envelope and poured everything out onto the desk. The sheriff was surprised to see the badge and some of his paperwork on the table and as he went through everything piece by piece, the look of surprise was on his face.

The sheriff looked up at Rachael. "Where did you find the badge and paperwork?"

"The Mexican girl had it with her when we found her."

The sheriff was in total disbelief, "Do you have any idea who the deputy is that is missing his badge?"

"Not yet; we were hoping you could tell us."

The sheriff looked at Buck. "You have any ideas?"

Buck shook his head no.

"This looks bad for my department to have a dirty cop on the payroll and be responsible for the death and torture of four Mexicans."

"I agree with you," Rachael replied.

"Let me take the evidence and I'll find out who it is," the sheriff suggested.

"I can't let you do that, simply because we, the FBI, found it and we need to have it in case we need it for trial," Rachael replied.

"Are you going to leave it here till it's needed?" the sheriff asked.

"No, we will take it with us and store the evidence in our Phoenix office."

"I think it would be safe here until it's needed for trial," the sheriff said.

Rachael at this time replied, "Rules are rules; you know how the FBI is about that kind of stuff."

The sheriff, realizing that there was no use pursuing the matter, asked, "When do you plan on moving the evidence to Phoenix?"

"Tomorrow morning; we have a special courier coming to pick it up."

"That's good."

All the time the conversation was going on Buck watched both the sheriff and the deputy, looking for some sign that would give away their thoughts. One thing for sure, the sheriff was cool and showed no emotion at all.

After a minute Buck said, "The deputy and I are going to stay the night to ensure that the evidence is handed off to the FBI tomorrow morning."

The sheriff looked at both of them. "That's a good idea; hope you get some sleep in the meantime."

Then added, "It's too late to drive home tonight, so I'm going to stay at the local hotel in town." And with that, he left.

After watching him leave, both Buck and Rachael let out a sigh of relief.

Buck looked at the deputy smiling, "You did good; you won't get shot tonight."

The deputy looked at him and said nothing.

Rachael looked at Buck. "You know he's coming back for the evidence?"

"Of course, I know he's coming back, the question is when tonight. How about we put the deputy near the front door tonight and we wait for him in the evidence room?"

"I don't trust the deputy all by himself out there. How about we have Evans or Foster out of sight watch over him? Kind of like what we did when we caught the deputy."

Buck smiled as Rachael dialed Foster and Evans on her phone. "You have a very distrustful mind, don't you?"

She smiled at Buck. "I trust you, I think."

After the phone calls were made, Foster and Evans came in and were briefed on the idea about catching the sheriff.

"I'll stay here out of sight and watch the deputy," Evans said.

"And I'll stake out the sheriff and let you know when he makes his move," said Foster.

With that done and organized, they all took their places and waited for the next move.

While Buck was sitting in the evidence room he asked Rachael, "Who do you think the sheriff is working for in this?"

"When we catch him, we'll ask him."

By now it was 10:30 pm and the office was locked for the evening. The town of New Rio was closed for the night, the café closed at 11:00 pm and their open sign was turned off, and a nightlight was the only light left on. Buck normally did his night rounds after the café was closed, but tonight would be different because of the evidence. The sheriff waited until midnight to make his move, knowing that Buck and the other deputy were the only ones inside the office. He knew it would be easy to get the evidence, especially with the deputy in there. He thought it would be as easy as pie getting the evidence and destroying all of it, including the paperwork. He stepped out of his hotel room and walked down the stairs past the lobby and the desk. It was quiet and no one was working the desk at this hour, so no one would see him leave through the front door. The sheriff started his car and slowing drove out of the parking lot towards town. Foster, who had been sitting in his car, saw him drive back to town and called Evans and let him know the sheriff was on the move. Evans passed the word to Rachael and Buck and, again, everybody got ready. The sheriff drove to the café and parked his car next to it. From there he walked to the sheriff's office, looked inside and saw the deputy sitting at the desk with a nightlight on reading.

He knocked on the door and the deputy jumped up, surprised at the knock, looked out the door recognizing the sheriff, opened the door and asked, "What can I do for you?"

"I've seemed to have left some papers here from earlier this evening, can I come in and get them?"

The deputy opened the door wider to let the sheriff in. "Sheriff, you want some coffee?"

The sheriff looked around and asked where Buck was. "I thought Buck was supposed to be here too," he said.

"I told Buck to go home; we didn't need two people to guard the evidence. So Buck left under protest and went home."

The sheriff smiled at this news. "Now we can get the evidence out of the back and destroy it and with the girl dead were clear. They can't prove our involvement with the murders or the drug money we got."

The deputy agreed and went back to the room where the evidence was and brought it out and handed it to the sheriff. With the evidence in his hand the sheriff looked at the deputy. "Only one last thing to do."

He drew his gun and pointed it at the deputy.

"It has to look like a break-in and I can't afford to have any witnesses saying I was here," the sheriff said.

With that said, the sheriff fired his weapon at the deputy hitting him in the shoulder.

Evans stood up and yelled, "Put your hands up, you're under arrest!"

The sheriff, surprised by Evans, turned to fire and shot again at Evans' voice.

Both Buck and Rachael came from the back room and yelled, "Put the gun down or we will shoot!"

The sheriff, realizing he was trapped, went for the door to escape; however, Foster, upon hearing the gunfire, covered the door and stood there waiting for the sheriff to step outside. When the sheriff appeared at the door, Foster fired his weapon, the bullet hitting the side of the building next to the door, intentionally missing the sheriff but letting him know there was no way out. At this point the sheriff, realizing there was nowhere to run or hide, laid his gun on the ground and stood there waiting for Buck to put handcuffs on him. Buck grabbed his hand and jerked it behind the sheriff's back. With Rachael and Evans covering him, Buck grabbed his other hand and slipped the other handcuff onto his wrist.

Buck looked at Rachael. "Two dirty cops in one night, that must be a record somewhere."

"Maybe you can be the sheriff now, seems as there are some positions opening up."

Foster went over to look at the deputy to see how he was doing, his wound was serious but he would live.

The ambulance arrived for the deputy, and as they carried him out on the gurney he looked up at Buck. "Whatever you want to know about all of this I'll tell you."

Buck looked at him and nodded his head in agreement.

"Get him outta here and good luck, deputy."

With that, they loaded him into the ambulance and off they went. Buck walked back to where they had the sheriff and leaned up against the wall, listening to Evans and Foster as they interrogated him.

Evans looked at the sheriff. "Two attempted murders, along with the four others in the cave, you're a real winner aren't you?"

The sheriff looked at him and laughed, "All you got on me is trying to steal the evidence."

"Don't forget about trying to kill the deputy."

"I can't believe I didn't kill him."

"The good news is he is alive and will testify against you," said Buck.

"Your days are numbered and you're going to jail for a long time."

The sheriff laughed at them again and said, "Do I look like I really care?"

Foster and Evans looked at him, along with Buck, and took him back to the holding cell and locked the door behind them.

When they were alone, Foster said, "That's one real badass. He will be hard to break, fortunately, the deputy is going to make it. With his testimony against the sheriff they're both going away for a long time."

Buck looked at them both, "Who would have thought that any of these guys were dirty? It makes me wonder who is clean in my department."

Foster looked at him in a meaningful way, "At least we know of one that is."

# CHAPTER XVI

Jim was waiting for the Monterrey Cartel's point man to contact him for the money drop he had gotten from the gangs in Southern California. While sitting in the shade near one of the misters in an open café his cell phone rang. He picked it up and answered it, "Yes."

The voice on the other end gave him a location to meet; with that he closed his cell phone, got up and walked out into the Arizona sunlight. He looked at his watch, it showed 10:30 a.m., and noticed it was already starting to get hot. Jim wondered how he had been able to handle the summers in Arizona. Of course, the standard answer was, "It was dry heat," the answer for everything in Arizona. He walked to his car, pulled out of the parking lot and got on the 101 loop and headed west towards downtown Mesa. As he drove, he got onto the interstate and continued west until he saw McClintock Blvd. and made for the exit. Turning right on the boulevard, he drove until he saw a Sonic Burger drive-in. He pulled into the last stall under the awning and waited. In about ten minutes another car pulled in opposite him on the other side. Jim waited to be sure these guys were the ones he was to meet. One of them got out of the car with a gym bag, and Jim got out of his car with the satchel full of money. Nothing was said between them, each took the other's bag and got into their cars and drove off. Short and sweet, the way Jim liked it to be. With the drugs, he was now ready to head back to Southern California to make another delivery to the gangs.

The cartel knew that Jim was their contact for the Chicago organization, and they also knew that up to this point Jim had been square in his dealings with them, no reason not to trust Jim so far. Now with a connection in Chicago the cartel was willing to expand the sales into that area. Chicago was fine with this, as long as they did the selling on the streets. The cartel said, as you wish, their main concern was the money generated from the extra sales of the drugs. Increased revenue meant more money for all who played the game. The drug distribution network in Chicago was pretty big and it was continuing to grow. The cartel wanted a piece of the action and was willing to deal with the devil, if necessary. When all was said and done, the money was worth what the cartel had to put up with from the gringos, leastwise until they figured out a way to move on without Chicago in the way. Up to now it was baby steps. Jim knew this alliance was tenuous at best, and it wouldn't take much for either the organization or the cartel to get ugly if either one of them was double-crossed. Jim was hoping for this and smiled to himself, knowing he would be the catalyst for this to happen.

First things first, Jim had to make another delivery to the gangs to pick up the money and head back, supposedly, to the cartel for delivery and more drugs. Then would be the time to contact Chicago and let them know all was going right for the takeover in California. Chicago would be pleased to know this. The time would come later to let the Mafia know about the hit on their compadres, who were intercepted before they could deliver the drugs. By telling the Mafia, it would allow them to set up a reprisal on Chicago. All in good time, all in good time, Jim kept saying to himself. Jim kept driving to California, knowing that this would be his last trip there before the gang war broke out. He smiled, knowing that in all gangs and cartels greed runs everything when it comes to power and money.

Once he got to California, he set up a meeting for the following day with the two gangs for delivery and money exchange. The gangs showed up as per agreement at the same place and time. Jim's team was also in place, waiting and watching out of sight, with the exception of the bodyguard. The gangs exchanged the money for the drugs, as done in the past, and left. This time Jim used his ear piece and told his team to follow the Firebirds gang. The distance for the Firebirds to travel was further and around other gang territories. With this in mind, Jim followed with his team to a somewhat remote area along the highway, waiting for the right time.

Using his sniper rifle, one of Jim's team took out the tire on the Cadillac. The car stopped and immediately the gang members quickly got out to fix the tire with the leader looking on.  The shot from the sniper rifle took the top of his head off, and he fell to the ground. The gang guards were taken out one by one till all were dead. The other two Cadillacs left in a hurry so as not to get shot, leaving the Cadillac and their leader and the other bodies with the flat all by itself.

Jim received the message that all was clear, drove his car up to the Cadillac and left a package he had picked up when he hit the Rollin' Thunders gang. This evidence would be the clincher that the Rollin' Thunders had done the hit. Jim got back into his car and said to himself, "Let the fun begin."

This time Jim took the money and the drugs and gave it to one of the team members to send to Chicago. One hour later Jim was on his way back to Arizona listening to some music on a CD, music that he and Karen listened to when hanging out together. For all of her faults, Jim and Karen loved each other very much. With that thought in mind, Jim turned up the music and cried for the first time since her death.

Jim made it to Phoenix about 10:00 pm, emotionally spent and also tired from driving. He found a hotel next to the freeway and paid to stay the night. When he got to his room, he turned on the TV and checked the news channel, hoping to hear something about the gang war in California. After about five minutes of watching, the news commentator spoke of a Cadillac being found with bodies all around it. The commentator explained the police were looking for anyone to come forward who may have seen the incident and asked them to call the local police department. The reporter who was with the police at the scene was asking the police officer what had happened.

"It looks like a hit from a rival gang here in the valley. We have found evidence to suggest this," the policeman said.

The officer showed evidence to the reporter and cameraman who was filming the interview for the TV station. Jim listened until the reporter sent it back to the newsroom when he was finished. Jim turned off the TV and went to bed.

As the news of another gangland hit was televised, agents Linda Sharp and Evans sat and wondered how the evidence was right on hand at the scene.

Evans spoke first. "Purely coincidental that they found evidence suggesting a gang hit, isn't it?"

Linda nodded in agreement. "Purely coincidental, I would like to see the evidence and check it out for myself."

Evans thought about what she said and agreed. "It would be interesting to check it out, and maybe we can get the local FBI office to run a diagnostics on it. I'll call them and see if they can look at it for us."

The Firebirds and the Rollin' Thunders saw the news as well, and when the evidence was shown to the reporter, both gangs knew what it meant. To them it meant war and the survivors would take over the other's turf and drug distribution network. Aside from the killing of their leaders, the prize was the full control of the drugs and the money. Blood for blood and eye for an eye was going to be the reply for their leaders' death.

Gearing up for the hit was on both gangs' minds; the weapons and location were next on the agenda. One way or another one gang would rule the turf and the business. To the gangs it was a matter of principle and right of conquest. As both gangs prepared for war, they sent out some of their soldiers to scout out the location of their enemy. As the Cadillacs made their way into the Rollin' Thunders' neighborhood, the dealers called the Rollin' Thunder headquarters to let them know. The Rollin Thunders prepared to meet them, by putting their soldiers out in front of the headquarters. When the Cadillac showed, the windows came down and the guns came up; the Firebirds would make it a drive-by attempt. The soldiers of the Rollin' Thunder saw the car coming and were ready for them. When they got to the building, they opened fired on the car. At first the bullets missed the car but one bullet found the engine, and it started to slow down and stop. With that the Firebirds got out of the car, firing at the soldiers in front of the building. Two of the Rollin' Thunder gang members fell where they had been hit. The Rollin' Thunder soldiers had both sides of the street covered and now the Firebird soldiers were caught in the crossfire. It was just a matter of minutes before all of the Firebird gang members were lying on the road dead. The Rollin' Thunder soldiers checked their fallen to see if they were alive. Of the two that fell one was dead and the other seriously wounded, he would later die on the way to the hospital.

When the police got there to ascertain what had happened, the four bodies of the

Firebird gang and the car were all they found. The police started their investigation by asking if anybody saw what happened in the area. Everybody claimed they were inside taking cover from the bullets and didn't see a thing. The CSI team looked at all of the brass lying on the ground and partially agreed with the police report. The first battle was over and the Rollin' Thunders claimed it as a win.

The police gang unit was out trying to find who started the war. The city of Los Angeles was on alert for the gang war. The LAPD was now aware of the gangs that were involved and they beefed up the patrols in both areas, hoping to stop any more violence from escalating between the two gangs. The Firebirds, upon learning what had happened to their soldiers, knew this meant a more deadly retaliation from their side. The one weapon they had was the RPG given to them by Jim. The RPG had two grenades left. This would be their answer to the first outcome of the battle. This time the Firebirds would catch the Rollin' Thunders celebrating their win out in the open. Then the RPG would speak for the Firebirds and the new designated leader knew where to find the Rollin' Thunders celebrating. Tonight would be the answer for today's loss. Tonight the Rollin' Thunders were in for a big surprise. The Firebirds laughed and carried on, knowing what was about to happen to the Rollin' Thunder, giving each other fist bumps and high fives, grabbing their ladies and drinking their beer and smoking their dope, getting ready to be the real men on the battlefield. Yes, tonight would be the night for the battle and all of the Firebirds celebrated, knowing that for some it would be their last night here on earth, knowing some would not return which made this celebration today all the more important for the Firebirds.

As in all wars, there are two facts that are consistent; that is, death and survivors. Those who die or survive will depend on their maker in heaven. As in all wars, there is a time to celebrate and a time to mourn; each time is always the same, before the battle begins and after the war is over. After searching for the survivors and burying the dead, sometimes the war will last for years, other times it would be for only a day. In either case, there would be death and survivors.

Another certainty in the world of the survivors and death is that it will always include the innocent, the collateral damage, the young and old, the newborn and the aged. These innocents will always bear the brunt of every war, every conquest of power, every fall of a civilization, every great upheaval started by man. Sometimes the innocent are lost in the turmoil and/or forgotten as time goes on, but will be remembered for their sacrifice by their families. The only other thing that is constant is the pain felt by the survivors and the innocents. The battle will continue until there is no one left on one side or the other or maybe both sides are gone; only time will tell.

Later that night, while the Rollin' Thunder were celebrating the win in the first battle, everybody seemed to be in a good mood. The music was loud and blaring and could be heard up and down the street. The sentries outside the house were celebrating too, probably too much, for they never saw the white Cadillac driving up the street. The Cadillac drove with its headlights off until about three houses down from the house of the Rollin' Thunder. Two of the Firebirds got out of the car and, carefully staying in the shadows of the houses, walked up to the house next door and fired the RPG into the house and then took off back to the car. When the shooters got to the Cadillac, it had turned around and was facing away from the house that now was on fire. The shock of the house being blown up caught everybody off guard, including the sentries outside. The blast knocked the sentries off their feet and onto the ground. One of the sentries raced into the house to do what he could, the other sentries were disoriented and confused by the blast. Looking around, they saw nothing, everyone still alive was screaming and yelling, some in pain, others in confusion. A secondary blast occurred when the main gas line leading into the house caught fire and blew up. By now only the sentries, who had moved away from the fire, were left alive. The house was a complete inferno of flames and smoke with no one inside surviving. The screaming and yelling were gone, with the exception of the sentries outside. When the fire department showed up to put out the fire the house was completely gone and all that was left to do was put out smoldering flames that were of no consequence.

The Firebirds had won the gang war for tonight; the body count, according to the news, was 15 people killed inside the house, burnt beyond recognition and no way to identify any of them. The fire department was able to contain the damage to one house by watering the houses next to it. It would be a while before the Rollin Thunder would be a threat to anyone in the neighborhood or, for that matter, to any gang in Los Angeles. This attack would now have a ripple effect on the other gangs wanting the territory left void by the Rollin' Thunder.

Who would win? For Jim it didn't matter; his part of it was complete, just a matter of time before the other gangs would fill in the hole. Jim heard the news the next day as he was getting ready to leave the hotel. His next step was to stop the mafia from delivering the money back to the cartel. He figured it would be in the hundreds of thousands of dollars he would take from the Mafia.

Knowing the route and time of the delivery was the key to intercepting the cartel's money which he had. Jim was acting in his own behalf this time, basically running rogue, and because of this he hired his own team to assist him in getting the money. Naturally, he would have to give some of the money to the team for their work, but to Jim it was worth it. Once again, the scenario would be to intercept all three cars and take the money but with nobody getting killed, unless it was necessary. At another spot in the road along the same highway the team of cars would have to be stopped. How this would be done was the long pole in the tent. Jim had thought about this for some time until he finally came up with an idea. He would stage an accident on the highway that would stop traffic long enough to grab the money and run. It would be pretty elaborate, yet it would work. His team got two wrecked cars and staged an accident on the highway. They also set up a tow truck and cleanup crew for the busted glass and other debris. With two flag people controlling traffic they could sort out which cars could go. On the day of the robbery Jim had the team in place and was waiting for the mafia cars to show.

Again, about 2:30 pm the first lead car showed. After flagging him down the car came to a stop. Waiting for the second car was only another five minutes. With both cars there the flagmen waited patiently for the third car to show. It wasn't long until the car appeared. Now, with all three cars sitting there the team moved in. They ordered everybody out of the cars and had them up against their cars, looking into the desert. Another two members of the team searched each one of the cars looking for the money. One of the searchers found it in the trunk of the second car. Jim showed up at this time from his lookout position carrying his 45 ACP with him, he grabbed the box of money and headed back to his perch. He also made sure that each driver and passenger saw his face. The driver of the second car he hit in the face with his gun to make sure the driver would re-member him. With that, the team gathered up the weapons the Mafia had and shot the left front tire of each car in case they had any ideas about getting the money back.

When Jim got the money and was away from the highway, he called his team to meet him at the designated place. About 20 minutes later the team showed up at the truck stop, and Jim paid out 50,000 dollars for their part in the heist, which would leave 200,000 dollars for his use. The team left and Jim put the box of money in the back of his car and headed to New Rio.

# CHAPTER XVII

Buck and Rachael walked into the office together about 9:00 am. Both were surprised to see each other running so late.

Buck held the door open for her saying, "Age before beauty."

She looked at him, smiling, "Don't you know beauty was a horse?"

This time Buck feigned the hurt look and then laughed. "Good one."

"Naturally."

With that, the day started with a brief by Linda Sharp, Jeff, and Wendy.

Evans started off by saying, "As you may not know, the gangs have been active in Southern California. The latest Intel says one of the gangs used an RPG to take out another gang's house in Los Angeles. The death count at this time is at least 15 in the house. No one really knows for sure because they haven't been able to identify the bodies, as they are burnt beyond recognition and, of course, none of the survivors are talking. The reason this is important is because of the use of an RPG, somebody supplied the RPG to the gang, and we're thinking this may be the tip of the iceberg. With that in mind, I now turn the time over to Linda."

Linda stood up. "We hope this is an isolated gang incident with the RPG, but we're not sure. As it stands, we think some other organization supplied the RPG to the gang, whether national or international we don't know. We have not heard any chatter about guns or weapons of any kind being stolen or sold to anyone in California. Bear in mind that doesn't mean it didn't happen; it just means we haven't heard about it."

"Linda, I think it did," Foster replied.

Linda nodded. "All we know is if this continues this will change everything when it comes to the gangs fighting over territory and distribution of whatever they want to sell. We have seen a push by some of the other gangs looking for more of this kind of firepower to use as a defense or maybe used for taking over another gang's territory. Nothing significant as of yet, but I know if I was one of the gang leaders, I'd be interested in getting my hands on some of this kind of hardware."

Buck leaned over to Rachael and whispered, "And the fun just keeps coming."

At this point Linda said, "I don't know what to tell you, other than keep your ears and eyes open for anything out of sorts, and please don't be stupid out there; the rules of the game may have changed."

Jeff and Wendy stood up after Linda finished her part of the brief. Jeff started the brief with maps showing where all of the drug cartels were located in Mexico with arrows showing their origin of growth and distribution from South America all the way into the U.S. The map showed the key cities where the drugs came into the country and where it went from there, mainly north and south to the big cities. New York, Chicago, Miami, Detroit, Los Angeles, and Salt Lake City were seen as the main hubs for delivery and from there dispersed by outlaw motorcycle gangs and street gangs to the smaller cities and towns throughout the nation. Another map showed where the drugs entered into New York from Europe via the golden triangle in Southeast Asia and Afghanistan and other parts of the Middle East. Another picture showed how the drugs moved through Miami via boats and submersibles from South America.

Jeff let the maps and photos do the talking for about a minute and said, "This is what we're up against and if you didn't know better it looks as if it is an all-out war where the bad guys are attacking from everywhere."

Foster and Evans both raised their hands at the same time; Jeff pointed at Evans. "Question?"

"Yes, are we winning this battle?" asked Evans.

Wendy looked at him. "What's your definition of winning? If you are asking are we controlling the flow or are we stopping it when it gets to the U.S., or do you mean are we catching the bad guys selling the stuff? If that's what you're asking, I'd say some days are good, some days are bad. That being said, should we legalize all of it or pretend it doesn't exist, you tell me. We, the government, have spent a lot of money trying to stem the tide. As you already know, the Monterrey Cartel is listed in the 50 richest businesses in the world with over three billion dollars in assets. For everyone we put out of business there is someone else who thinks he is smarter and tougher than the last guy who got caught who is willing to start all over again. The lure of easy money and lots of it will always be a temptation for the lazy, greedy, or the smart people in the world."

Jeff then put up a slide showing the laundering of money from cartels to the world-wide banks back to the cartels through companies that were legal."

Everybody who was in the briefing just sat there mesmerized and kept looking at the pictures and slides.

Wendy continued, "It's like cancer. We can cut or operate on it or we use therapy to kill the cancer. As you know, sometimes it works, sometimes it doesn't. But if we don't try and stop the cancer, we die anyway. You tell me if it's worth it."

All were still quiet, and with that, both Jeff and Wendy said, "As for our particular problem, we haven't heard anything from our sources concerning the Monterrey Cartel. The cartels tend to take care of their own problems their special way. We usually get the information after the fact or when something has already happened. We look for trends and listen to the chatter and watch the borders with the help of the US Air Force, Marines, Coast Guard, and Immigration Naturalization Service (INS). Again, sometimes we're right and sometimes we're wrong."

With that, Jeff and Wendy sat down leaving the slides, pictures, and maps on the board.

Evans stood up. "This brief was to let you know not just what we are up against but also to know what questions to ask when you interrogate the bad guys. With that thought in mind, has anybody heard how the deputy is doing?"

"He's willing to talk ever since his boss tried to kill him," Buck replied.

"Duh," Evans smiled.

Everybody laughed at this, setting the mood back to a somewhat more palatable atmosphere.

Evans looked at Foster and Rachael saying, "You get first crack at the deputy."

They both nodded and stood up to leave. Buck stood up as well. "What about me?"

"We're going to soften him up for you first," Evans said.

Buck stood there a moment and smiled at Foster and Rachael. "Be gentle with him now, ya hear?"

Rachael and Foster smirked and both said at the same time, "Oh, we will."

With that, Buck went out to the street and down to the café and got an order of coffee for the whole team to go. As he stood waiting for his order, a thought came to him about the sheriff. He had to be working with someone in the drug business, someone who would lead them to the FBI and to the next level up and, hopefully, even higher up the food chain. When Buck returned to the office with the coffee, he approached Evans about what he was thinking.

Evans listened. "We've already started looking into his financial records and anything else we can think of, but as it stands, he's clean."

Buck thought a moment before speaking out loud to Evans. "The sheriff is too smart to have records of his money for drugs lying around, especially in his bank account. He would have it hiding somewhere else under a different name or maybe a joint account with someone he trusts."

Evans agreed with Buck and called his counterparts in Phoenix to do a thorough background check on the sheriff and look for a family member or friend he is in contact with either by letter, texting, e-mail or phone records.

When Evans was done with the call, he looked at Buck. "You know you would make a good agent for the FBI, especially bringing good coffee."

Buck accepted the compliment and smiled and thanked him.

"You know what they say about being a government worker? It's bad enough I work for the state and county."

Evans laughed, took his coffee and walked over to where Jeff and Wendy were looking at some papers.

Foster came out of the interrogation room, surprised that the only person the deputy would talk to was Buck. Foster said, looking at Buck, "You guys must be great friends."

Buck looked surprised. "Where did you get that idea?"

"He won't talk to anybody but you."

"It must be my bedside manner that he likes."

At that, Buck walked into the interrogation room where Rachael was keeping an eye on the deputy. "What's up?"

Rachael asked the deputy, "Do you mind if I stay and listen?"

"No problem, I just want have somebody I trust in here with me," the deputy said.

The deputy started to say something and Buck cut him off. "I want to know how you first got into bed with the sheriff?"

The deputy looked at him for a moment. "The sheriff found that I had child porn on my computer at home; he had traced it from my computer at work. I thought for sure I would lose my job because of it. I was surprised when he said not to worry about it. At first I didn't know what to think. I thought he was lying to me. But nothing ever came of it. The fact is he started having me go with him every-where, even when it came to getting the money from the drug dealers. He knew where they were hanging and he would find them and shake them down for the money, threatening to kill them or lock them up."

Rachael looked at Buck. "I didn't know you had dealers in New Rio."

"Not just here, all through the county."

Buck looked at the deputy. "How long has this been going on?"

"About six years now."

"Continue," Buck said.

The deputy went on, "Pretty soon I was assisting the sheriff in the shakedowns all by myself. I would get the money and deliver it to him and he would start splitting the money with me. After a while we got the idea instead of going after the dealers, we thought, why not go after the distributors and make more money? So we went after the dealers to find out when the drugs were being delivered and waited to catch the distributors red-handed. When we did, we made a deal with the cartel's people and started making a lot of money. All we had to do is guarantee safe passage through the county for delivery. The cartel increased the amount of drugs that were coming in and we made the money from it."

"How much money are we talking about?" Rachael asked.

"About 10,000 dollars each for every delivery, which was twice a month."

"Where did you hide the money that you received?" Buck asked.

"We knew we would get caught if we used a bank account to hold the money for us. So what we did was we put the money into an offshore bank in one of the Caribbean islands. Pretty soon when the other cartels wanted to cut into the business of the cartel we were assisting, they would ask us to take care of the problem for them.

"To include killing?" Rachael asked

The deputy looked at her and nodded his head yes. "The desert can hide a lot of things you don't want found."

"Can you tell us where the bodies are at?" Buck asked.

"Yes, if you give me a pad of paper and a pen, I'll write down the locations for you."

Buck looked at him. "How many burials are we talking about?"

"At least a dozen or so, maybe more."

By now both Buck and Rachael had to take a break from the interrogation of the deputy.

"I need you to show me where the places are on a map. But before you do let me get some paper and the map first; that way we are all on the same page," Buck said.

The deputy agreed with Buck's request and waited for Buck to get everything. When Buck walked out to get the paper, he signaled Evans and Foster, "Go into the identity room and listen to what is going on."

Evans and Foster, along with Linda, Jeff, and Wendy, went into the room and waited. Buck returned with the paper and map for the deputy to show and write everything down.

The deputy looked at Buck. "I want something in return for what I'm about to show and tell you."

Buck looked at Rachael and wondered what the deal could be.

"At this point we can offer you life in club fed and serve it in Florida," Rachael said.

"Put it in writing and for how long?"

"We will need to talk to the district attorney about that."

The deputy looked at her. "As an act of good faith, I will show you one place out there in the desert where you can see our handiwork."

Evans came into the room. "Show me on the map and we'll go from there."

The deputy looked at the map for a minute and got his bearings and traced the map with his finger following a road from the town where the sheriff's headquarters was located.

After two minutes of looking at the map he said, "Right here is where you will find some bodies."

With that information Evans left the room and called the FBI in Phoenix and checked to see if they knew of any police departments with cadaver dogs and then placed a call to the district attorney. While Evans was checking things out, Buck looked at the deputy. "Why did you do it?"

The deputy looked at Buck, surprised by his question. "We were killing two birds with one stone. We controlled what was going on in the county and getting rid of the trash making the county safe. We thought we were doing the right thing and making some money on top of that."

"Start writing," Buck said.

To which the deputy proceeded to write about what he had said previously. Foster, who had been listening to all of this in the other room, said to the others, "Looks like we're going for a ride out into the desert today."

"What about the sheriff, should we take him along for the ride too?" Linda asked.

"We need to check with Evans on that one."

In about 30 minutes the deputy put down the pen and looked up at Buck.

"When I get it writing about where I'm going to spend the rest of my life, you'll get more. One thing I will tell you is that we were only the little fish in the pond; there were others involved in this as well, higher up the chain."

Buck looked surprised at the statement. The deputy, seeing his surprise, laughed at him.

"Do you think we could do all of this all by ourselves?"

The deputy shook his head in bewilderment at how naive Buck had been.

Later in the afternoon the trip was set up to go find the bodies that the deputy had shown on the map. Evans and Foster rode in the first SUV with the deputy handcuffed and shackled in the back seat. Buck rode with Rachael and Linda in the second SUV. The cadaver dog and owner rode in their own truck, as well as, the digging team. With the deputy giving directions to the site everybody followed the first SUV. An hour later the deputy got out of the truck and looked the terrain over, trying to remember where he was. After looking for about five minutes he pointed his finger and said it's over there. They drove about ten more minutes and stopped at the deputy's request. The cadaver dog was brought out and the owner started doing a search of the area with the dog. In a short time the dog alerted on a small mound next to a rock outcropping. The digging team started to dig. After some time had passed one of the diggers found what appeared to be a skull and some bones about two feet down. After cordoning off the area the diggers continued digging and expanded the area by about ten feet in all directions. After an hour they found the remains of two bodies.

When asked who they were the deputy said, "Mules, just mules. We took the drugs and whatever they had of value and buried them here."

"How did you know they were working with another cartel?" asked Foster.

"We had followed them from the border and after hearing some gunshots we tracked them to here."

"Gunshots?"

"Yeah."

"We figured these two killed the other mules from the cartel we were working for and robbed them for the drugs and left the bodies on the other side of the Mexican border."

At 6:00 pm the diggers found all of the bones in the pit and the forensics team was called out. When they were finished taking pictures and identifying the bones, the forensics lead said, "As far as we are concerned, we will gather up the bones and anything else we find and take them to

Phoenix for proper identification and storage. Your work here is done; ours is about to start once we're back at the lab."

With that, Evans and Foster put the deputy back into the SUV and headed back to New Rio. Buck and Rachael headed back as well. Linda stayed as oversight on the dig.

The ride back for Rachael and Buck was pretty quiet, not much to say about the day's work. Both were tired and worn out from being in the sun all day.

When they checked into the office, Evans was on the phone talking to the District Attorney. After telling him about the bodies the deputy had led them to, the district attorney agreed that the offer of club fed would stand for the deputy. Buck was made aware of this and told the deputy that it was agreed to by the district attorney.

Now that Rachael was with him in the interrogation room and a video camera was set up, along with a tape recorder, they began a more thorough interview. The deputy outlined the organization of the drug business from the county attorney all the way down to the deputies in the office. He also included how they got rid of evidence and put evidence in place to blackmail the ones who didn't want to go along. The sheriff worked with the county attorney in the day-to-day operations of the drug smuggling and enforcement. The deputy showed them on the map several more areas where bodies could be found and where they kept the drugs and money that couldn't ship overseas.

It was about 2:00 am when they took their first break from the interview. Both Rachael and Buck were astounded by how large the network was and how efficient they had been hiding it. When they apprised Evans and Foster about what they had learned from the deputy, Evans and Foster both started getting search warrants to go after the players, especially the county attorney. They had to come up with a story as to why the sheriff hadn't been in his office for the last couple of days so as not to arouse suspicion. Foster and Evans used the story that he had taken some time off for a break to get away for a while. That story in place, the FBI and state police sent more people to the county seat to start their investigations into the sheriff's organization as to who was involved in the drug business.

The FBI raided the sheriff's and the county attorney's offices, confiscating their computers. The FBI team came out with boxes of paperwork and anything they thought would have information that would prove their involvement in the wrongdoing. The county attorney was upset that he was being investigated and as they led him out of the office handcuffed, he bowed his head and said, "I want a lawyer." With the sheriff and the county attorney behind bars and everyone else involved being rounded up, the county office looked pretty empty to the deputies who worked there. The entire secretarial staff that worked in the building were in a complete state of shock. They didn't know what to do, as their computers had been taken as well. There was a team of agents who were there to talk to the secretaries as well.

When the news hit the papers, the reporters had their equipment set up outside the county building, watching and waiting to talk to someone about what was going on. The FBI handled the press and occasionally would go out and update them on their findings, all in all big news for a quiet county. The press showed the picture of the deputies being led out from the building into waiting SUVs with U.S. Marshals escorting them. The press was having a heyday with all of this, especially the big players like the sheriff and his lieutenants and captains. All of the key players that were apprehended were interviewed by both state and FBI personnel. The hours of interviews would take weeks to organize and put down on paper everything that was asked and said by the guilty. All the while more bodies were being discovered out in the desert.

Buck and the team stood back and watched the media circus, smiling that they found a chink in the armor of the cartels. Jeff and Wendy started hearing the groans from the radio chatter at their Intel posts. The Monterrey Cartel was doing damage control for their distribution network, hoping not get indicted by the FBI for their part in this investigation. The last thing the cartel needed was to be indicted by the FBI, there would be no stopping the U.S. government from coming after them, especially the DEA. The cartel burned their own contacts inside and outside the cartel in the United States and Mexico as well. The body count was getting higher and the agencies were going after anybody who would talk to them about the drug operations in the U.S. What began as a routine investigation of a bank robbery and murders now turned into a manhunt against the cartel and their network.

The sheriff, seeing what was going on, decided to start talking in hopes of a deal to keep him from a death sentence. The Feds were not as open to that possibility as they were with the deputy. The feds offered the sheriff life in prison at a maximum security prison with solitary confinement from the regular population. Realizing he had no other options he took the deal. The sheriff confirmed what the deputy had already told them about other players on the other side of the border who were involved with the drug trade, including a key member of the Mexican drug counterterrorism unit. The DEA and the Mexican state police would be notified of this new information.

The Mafia who moved the drugs were rounded up and sent to the police departments that had room in their jails to hold them until they could be processed into the federal prisons. The ripple effect went all the way up to the governor's office, with the assistant to the governor being arrested for taking money from the cartel for political favors.

Wendy looked at Rachael, Foster, and the rest of the team. "We won this one. After the fallout from this, the whole system will have to be vetted again in case we missed somebody."

Buck went back to the deputy, who was still being held in their jail and asked, "Do you happen to know about a guy named Jim Olds?"

"We knew of him only by his wife who was one of the people that got killed in the bank robbery. Occasionally, we would use him to move a small amount of drugs to California. He wasn't a real player in the grand scheme of things. We heard rumors that he was tied with the Chicago organization but could never prove it," the deputy replied.

"What do you know about the local bank being used for money laundering?"

The deputy looked surprised by the question. "You got me; most of the money being laundered for the cartel was in Phoenix and other bigger city banks."

He stopped midway and chuckled at the prospect that the local bank was being used for dirty money and laughed out loud. "It just goes to prove that there are a lot of greedy people out there."

Buck stood there and didn't know what to say about his comment. At this, Buck wasn't sure of where to go or what to do, as far as Jim was concerned. He found Rachael and told her the news about Jim.

"We can put a BOLO out for Jim; maybe we will get lucky and catch him," Rachael said.

Buck smiled. "Forever the optimist."

"Well, ya never know what will happen."

Buck would have been surprised to know how close Jim really was to them at this point in time.

Buck took Rachael to lunch at the café and just sat there, enjoying the coolness of the room. It would be later, after everything was complete, that Buck would take her to the waterfall again for a picnic and propose to her there. She would accept the proposal and ask, "What took you so long?"

Buck chuckled and stood there with a look of, "How did you know I would ask?"

Later when she told Foster and Evans about the upcoming marriage, they said,

"We knew it all along, and it's about time."

Buck couldn't understand how everybody else knew except him.

Jim had seen the headlines in the paper about the sheriff and others being busted for their part in the cartel's drug business. He was glad he wasn't more involved with that mess. Once the cartel realized they had been ripped off by the Chicago organization, the cartel would take action, but only after the smoke cleared from the current goings-on. Jim decided right then and there his vengeance for the death of his wife was paid in full. With that, he could move on with the money from the holdup. Maybe with some luck the cartel wouldn't miss it too much with everything else going on.

Jim smiled at the idea of getting away with murder; this was right in his eyes for his beloved Karen. As he stood looking at the headstone by her gravesite, he knelt down and placed a flower at the base of the headstone and got up and walked away. His boy would be raised by his sister in Phoenix as she was the closest relative the boy had. The sister and her husband were good people and were unable to have their own children, and they would love the boy as if he were their own child. That would be the right thing for his son. The other alternative for the boy would be always on the run with no end in sight. One day in the future Jim would contact his sister to have her send the boy back to him, but for now it was better this way for all concerned.

Jim got into his car and headed south to the border to catch a flight to go to a country without extradition agreements with America.

# EPILOGUE

The fallout from the case against the Smith County Sheriff's Department was huge. The recall election was a landslide vote for Buck to be the sheriff and major reorganization of the department. There would be new deputies with new faces including a female captain who had crossed over from the FBI to help run things.

The case of the robbery/murders is still open but has gone cold; it will stay open for the next ten years or so. The case never left the minds of the sheriff or his captain, and they thought about it every so often.

The cartel, upon realizing they had been ripped off by the organization, went after them. They started by taking out the drug dealers and then went after the bookies, the prostitutes and the meth labs. From there the cartel went after the leadership of the organization. This proved to be a mistake for the cartel. Other organizations within Chicago and with the help of the police and FBI retaliated in kind against the cartel. Now the kingpin of the cartel was on the run and hiding from the Mexican army and DEA. None of the cartel people sent to Chicago survived, and the ones that did are in Joliet State Prison for the long haul. The organization would never rise up to be the power they had been before the cartel business. The favors that had been given freely had come at a cost to their empire. As far as the Chicago organization was concerned, Jim Olds had a 250,000 dollar reward out on his head saying wanted dead or alive.

The Southern California gangs split the territory of the Firebirds and Rollin' Thunder between themselves and were more powerful than the Firebirds and the Rollin Thunder. The territory was swallowed up into the vacuum and the Firebirds and the Rollin' Thunder had ceased to exist. The fighting would last another six months and the body count would be relatively small, compared to what it could've been. The police and other agencies stepped in to keep it from getting any higher. But, in the end it was business as usual, just under new management.

Evans was promoted and transferred to Miami, dealing strictly with the cartels and drug running. Foster was promoted as well for his work and became second in command over the state police and is now working eight to five, five days a week, allowing him time to go fishing with his family on the weekends. Linda was given the opportunity to work with Evans in Miami, which she gladly took to get away from the high cost of living in California.

Jeff and Wendy were given letters of appreciation for their part in stopping the Monterrey Cartel. They were transferred later with a promotion to work in Washington DC at DEA headquarters.

Jim Olds was never found again; rumors are that he was reunited with his son after being absent for about six years. Where they are is anybody's guess.

www.ingramcontent.com/pod-product-compliance
Lightning Source LLC
Chambersburg PA
CBHW030016180626
46810CB00001B/69